Murder by the Minutes

A Piper O'Donnell Social Lite Mystery

by

Jennifer Vido

Copyright 2015 by Jennifer Vido

For information, email **Cozy Cat Press**, cozycatpress@aol.com or visit our website at: www.cozycatpress.com

COZY CAT
P R E S S

ISBN: 978-1-939816-59-7

Printed in the United States of America

Cover design by Paula Ellenberger
http://www.paulaellenberger.com/

1 2 3 4 5 6 7 8 9 10

Dedication
For my parents, Diane and Jack Plisky, and my two
brothers, John and Jim

Acknowledgments

For ten years, I had the privilege of serving on the
Board of Trustees of the Harford County Public
Library. I continue to be in awe of its steadfast
dedication to our community. Thank you to Mary
Hastler, Jennifer Ralston, and my friends at HCPL for
your support of my writing career. To my plot sisters
Denise Holcomb, Sally LeSage, Liz Murphy, and Karen
Traskey, who read early drafts of this manuscript, thank
you for your encouragement and sage advice. This book
would still be in draft form if it weren't for the gentle
nudges from Judy Hunt. Thank you for not giving up on
me. To my arthritis swim class who makes each
morning brighter, I treasure your love and friendship.
To Toni Haigley and Anna Pearce...thanks for always
being there. To the Bakers, DeMaries, Pliskys, and
Vidos, thank you for being my biggest fans. To my
faithful writing companion and rescue dog Charlie, I hit
the doggie lottery when I found you. And finally, to my
husband Durbin and our two sons, Henry and Sam,
thanks for loving Piper *almost* as much as I do. I love
you with all of my heart.

Also by Jennifer Vido:

Country Clubbed

Par for the Course

Cast of Characters

Piper O'Donnell—socialite in search of happily-ever-after

Judge Denise Halbreath—county judge

Chuck Loudon—proprietor of the local hardware store

Carolyn DeWitt—queen bee of the country club

Larry Flagstone—library director

Brandt Dixon—local art dealer

Mrs. B.—executive assistant

January Mitchell—town hippie

Rev. Stephen Black—United Methodist minister

Desiree Hamilton—information technology specialist

Nancy—president of the Library Friends group

Jim Wagner—general contractor

Penelope Davenport—Piper's little sister

Rusty O'Brien—Piper's love interest

Helen Morgan—Rusty's mother

Capt. Morgan—local law enforcement

Jay Baker—beat reporter

Shep Stewart—Main Street gallery co-owner

Mrs. Johnson—librarian in charge

Chapter 1
Call to Order

"If we plan on making this library ball a huge success, the tickets will need to go on sale sooner rather than later," insisted the vivacious blonde draped in an exquisite pink designer suit. She sashayed to the other side of the room in her killer stilettos with the unwavering precision of a high-end fashion model. "I'm not sure what all the fuss is about concerning the minor details. That's exactly why we established all of these committees." Piper drew the group's attention to the white board affixed on the wall by intentionally flashing her sparkling diamond engagement ring. "It gives the Library Friends ample opportunity to put their stamp on the event. Remember…" she clasped her perfectly manicured hands together, "this is a community effort, my fellow board members." With a sunshiny grin, she surveyed the group assembled around the boardroom table for their reaction as she slowly took her seat. Their solemn faces did little to indicate a ringing endorsement for Piper's proposal causing her to stash the latest celebrity magazine under her stack of board notes. Perhaps the party planning issue would not be needed just yet.

Piper O'Donnell reveled in her highly controversial appointment to the Woodlawn Library Board of Trustees. Despite having resided in the quaint Ohioan suburb of Woodlawn for more than a few years, Piper would forever be labeled as a scheming gatecrasher. This well-known fact did little to deter the charismatic trustee from making her mark on the town. An active board member, she boasted a perfect record of attendance for every function, obligatory as well as optional. This lavish event would mark her one year anniversary on the board, a fact she proudly repeated when given the chance. Being the brainchild behind this soiree was a feather in her cap. Piper's vision to make the library ball the social event of the season was the driving force behind her dogged determination. Of course, the chance to showcase a stunning gown to her infamous circle of friends was all the incentive she needed. Fashion would always remain Piper's first love.

Judge Denise Halbreath peered above her tortoise spectacles in order to catch Piper's eye. Her notorious stare was known to make hardened criminals tremble when awaiting a verdict. Not so much for Piper. The so-called firecracker trustee with a plucky disposition took this as a good sign and returned the fire-breathing judge's gaze with a noticeable wink and a thumbs-up. Over the past year, the judge tended to favor Piper's unconventional proposals and somewhat flagrant opinions more times than not. Piper chalked it up to the judge's need to appear confident among her peers with her bold move to endorse Piper's nomination. Whether that merited any truth didn't matter. As far as Piper was concerned, her five year appointment was the best decision the judge had ever made.

"Are we about done with this meeting? We don't need to confer over every minute detail. I have an early tee time in the morning, people," Chuck Loudon grumbled. The burly six-foot tall hardware store owner with dark hair and a bellowing voice had no patience for idle chit-chat. He was notorious for cutting people off mid-sentence in an effort to get to the greens. Married to a trendy hair stylist who spent the majority of her day in a *Bravo* television induced haze, the two were a mismatched pair.

"Not yet, Chuck," Carolyn DeWitt chided him. As the reigning socialite of the country club, the snooty bottle blonde was used to getting her way. A newbie on the board due to a trustee's unexpected job transfer out of state, she was anxious to call the shots. When the selection committee went to task to fill the vacant seat, Carolyn was the unanimous choice. Needless to say, had Piper served on that particular committee, the results would not have favored Carolyn. The two were social frenemies at best.

Ms. Fancy Pants, as Piper liked to call her, inserted herself into the discussion whenever possible, whatever the topic. It truly didn't matter. Like a petulant child vying for her mother's attention, Carolyn needed to be acknowledged. "We need to commit to a theme before moving forward. I agree with Piper."

Astonished to have Carolyn's support, Piper did her best to appear appreciative.

Carolyn continued, "The tickets do need to go on sale. The event is less than a month away. With the opening of golf season, social calendars will start filling up. We also need to vote on the theme. It's Monday already. Another week has gone by without any decisions being made." Dressed in a pale yellow designer sheath mirroring the shade of her perfectly coiffed hair, Carolyn tilted her head to the right while gently caressing her milky white strand of pearls. Her facial expressions were difficult to read due to an abundance of Botox and fillers regularly inserted into her face, a hot topic whispered among the ladies.

The board consisted of seven members—four women and three men. The current library director, Larry Flagstone, a non-voting member of the board, favored women due to his single status. An out-of-shape divorcé sporting a blatant comb-over, he wasn't what one would call a catch. According to the literary genius, as he so named himself, stacking the board with women increased his odds of being kept abreast of the local rumor mill. The gap-toothed leader often bragged that news of a pending divorce was more effective on the dating scene than using Match.com. So far, his results did not support his self-inflated ego. "I agree with Chuck. We need to wrap things up," Larry concurred. "It's almost eight o'clock." He made a point of verifying it by consulting his mammoth-sized wristwatch. Among other things, his vanity kept him from succumbing to his desperate need for eyewear.

"I make a motion that we accept my novel idea for the Pink Library Ball." Piper made quote signs with her fingers to emphasize the word *pink*. "Now that it's springtime, we can take advantage of the gorgeous flowers in bloom." She turned her gaze towards Brandt Dixon, the current president of the board, for approval and then mimicked a pad and pen to Mrs. B., the director's executive assistant, for her to record the motion.

Mrs. B. served as the eyes and ears of the library. If something was going on in the stacks, she knew about it. Per usual, the willful taskmaster was primly attired in a pink floral blouse, beige polyester slacks, and taupe shoes. Dangling around her neck was a pair of purple colored cat's-eye glasses firmly attached to a long, bedazzled chain. Her taut gray hair rested neatly atop her head in a beehive inspired hairdo. Larry himself had suitably given her the nickname, Mrs. B. Her proper last name remained a mystery.

Brandt did not endorse nor reject Piper's motion, causing the others to follow suit. A quiet man with broad shoulders and flaming red hair, he stood a mere five-foot-eight. His simple, yet classic pinstripe suit contributed to his fastidious presence. An art dealer by trade, he and his partner owned a small gallery on Main Street near the local diner. Serving his last year on the board, Brandt took great pride in the legacy he would leave behind. Over the last few months, he had become quite sentimental when it came to meetings or press junkets he would no longer have the privilege of attending. The library ball had the potential to make or break his philanthropic career, a consideration he did not take lightly. Before he could speak, January Mitchell swooped in.

"I propose we have a green ball this year." The total antithesis of Piper, Jan donned a long, flowery skirt matched with a poufy avocado blouse. The only accoutrement with any semblance of business attire was an organic cotton scarf loosely tied around her neck. Her cropped white mane complimented her piercing emerald eyes, while the peace signs hanging from her ears served as billboards for her personal beliefs.

Piper tapped her temple in deep thought. "Fine," she blurted. "Jan, if we must use your signature color, then let's compromise. Pink and green go well together. Just ask the folks at Lilly Pulitzer." Piper laughed at her own little joke.

Judge Halbreath and Carolyn gazed at each other, eyebrows aloft.

"I meant green, as in environmentally-conscious. Recycled paper products. Plants instead of flowers." Jan's condescending tone did little to ruffle Piper.

"Of course! I get your point, but I'm not sure asking the guests to reuse the same plate and cup all night will attract the kind of numbers we were hoping for," Piper winced.

The group took a collective moment to digest what was said. Mrs. B. fiddled with the ornate button on her flowery blouse.

"Why don't we forget the color schemes and stick to a simple Black & White Ball?" suggested Reverend Black, the sexy pastor at the Woodlawn United Methodist Church. The strapping gent was fodder for many a conversation at the country club. Single, and so, so hot, this devout man of the cloth had a way of making even the staunchest of atheists into a believer. Perhaps one of the most desirable bachelors in town, this fortysomething hunk with salt and pepper hair was used to wielding his influence over others. Measuring an impressive six-foot-three, his presence was hard to miss.

"Hold on, Mr. Holy Roller!" Piper had a distinct way with words. "No disrespect intended." She qualified her response.

"None taken," he bounced back. His devilish grin appeared somewhat sacrilegious.

"Good. Now, listen here. That's unfair. Just because your name is Black doesn't mean that you get to have your own ball." She nodded at Carolyn. "Back me up here, girlfriend."

Carolyn made a croaking sound.

"I take that as a no," Piper replied. She anxiously twisted her long blonde hair around her finger as she weighed her options.

Brandt instantly tensed up. Despite being their leader, the mere hint of confrontation manifested itself with hot sweats and an immediate nervous tick. "Judge Halbreath? Do you have any suggestions?" he fanned himself with last month's minutes.

Denise Halbreath was caught off-guard as was evident by the need for Brandt to call her name twice. With all eyes upon her, she subtly tossed her phone in her opened satchel and took a deep breath. Her reluctance to immediately address the group prompted

Brandt to sneak a quick puff from his asthma inhaler. It was obvious to see the stress was getting to him.

Larry stepped right in and took control of the situation. "As library director, I will have the final say concerning the theme." His upright posture demanded their attention.

"Who put you in charge?" Jan challenged his authority.

His rigid frame suddenly went limp. As Larry struggled to break free from his chair, the plastered strands of hair from his comb-over inadvertently flopped forward. Instantly, his obstructed vision threw him off-balance and he fell forward. The end result was less than flattering as the board couldn't help but fixate on his motionless figure lying face down on the carpeted floor.

"While you pull yourself together, let's try once more to brainstorm," suggested Denise. Her attempt to be diplomatic was marginal at best. She made no bones about her distaste for Larry Flagstone.

With the clock ticking, Chuck made a rare move to engage in the discussion. "To be fair to everyone present at this table, and those on the floor," his voice trailed off.

"Real funny," countered Larry. He repositioned his hair, brushed himself off, and then returned to his seat.

"Let's not quibble over details. How about something simple like...Khakis and Cocktails?" Chuck volunteered.

Piper choked on her water. "You think?" she managed to spit out.

Chuck fiddled with his ballpoint pen. "Why not? What man doesn't own a good pair of khakis? And, who doesn't enjoy a cocktail?"

The men nodded their head in agreement. He did have a point. Chuck's suggestion seemed to have calmed Brandt's nerves for the moment.

Piper was not giving up that easily. "Brandt, what if we showcased some of the up and coming local artists that you feature in your gallery?"

Her animated speech garnered their attention.

"We could auction off selected works, and a portion from the sales would be donated back to the library." Piper's overture was met with interested nods.

"Keep talking," Jan said. For once, the two shared a harmonious moment.

Piper liked what she was hearing. "We could call the event Art & Sold. Kinda like *heart and soul*, but with a twist." She pointed out to Jan, "Even has a hippy-ish ring to it."

Denise nodded her head. "Let's mull that over for minute. I think it could potentially work."

Reverend Black was not swayed by her artsy proposal.

"It's an admirable proposition; however, I think we're losing sight of what our true intentions need to be. This event is to raise funds for the library for books, not paintings. Organizing a massive art show would be quite the undertaking. I agree with Chuck in the sense that less is more. I propose we name it Booklovers' Ball. Isn't that what it is?" Reverend Black rested his case.

Carolyn added her two cents. "What if we combined both of your ideas into one? Booklovers' Ball: Art & Sold?" She gestured towards Jan for confirmation.

"I like it!" Jan concurred. "Perhaps we could re-title some of the pieces after great works of literature."

Piper said, "Like if the canvas depicts a bucolic countryside, we could label it *The Tale of Jemima Puddle-Duck* from Beatrix Potter. Brandt, you'd be perfect for that job since you are well-versed in both areas."

"*Jemima Puddle-Duck*? That's the best you could do? I think Jan was referring to something along the lines of *The Great Gatsby* or *A Tale of Two Cities*," chided Carolyn.

Piper looked annoyed. "It would certainly appeal to the masses especially for those mothers who actually read to their children rather than delegating the responsibility to their nannies. Yes, I do believe they would relate just fine." Her obvious dig was duly noted by all assembled.

"Well, then," Carolyn proceeded, "I agree Brandt is best suited for that responsibility. Moving on." The grandiose wave of her hand appeared to put an end to the uncomfortable exchange. "Have we given any thought to implementing online registration? It's fast, convenient, and practical for us busy moms on-the-go." She tried to redeem herself in the eyes of her peers.

As usual, Piper couldn't help herself. "I emphatically agree. While at the salon, *busy* moms like Carolyn would be able to purchase tickets with just one click of their iPhones. Larry, do we have the technology available to make this a reality?" While turning her head in his direction, she gave a private nod to Carolyn as if saying touché.

Despite his embarrassing mishap, Larry was quick to jump into the fray. "Yes, we do. Our savvy information technology expert Desiree Hamilton spearheaded the project. We are now able to collect fines and fees 24/7. Last month we saw a marked increase of approximately 40% in collected revenue. Desiree projects…"

"A lot of information we don't need to know at this juncture." Leave it to Chuck to rain on Larry's parade. "A simple *yes* or *no* would suffice," he huffed in frustration.

Jan patted the impatient Chuck on the forearm in a sympathetic gesture of camaraderie. It was a well-known fact Larry had the hots for his subordinate. A real no-no for the man in charge, yet Larry continued to pursue the twenty-something beauty.

Denise finally decided to weigh in. "Thank you, Larry for that information. I make a motion we accept Booklovers' Ball: Art & Sold for the theme. I also propose we make it as environmentally friendly as possible and only use Evites. That will give Desiree an opportunity to show off her myriad of skills." She smiled at Larry who appeared well-pleased with her suggestion.

Brandt said, "Do I have a second?"

"So moved!" affirmed Piper and Carolyn at the same time. The ladies eyed each other from across the mahogany table.

Mrs. B. stated, "Piper seconded it." She smiled sideways at Piper.

Carolyn's exaggerated sigh confirmed her displeasure of Mrs. B.'s assertion.

"All in favor?" he called for a vote.

The group responded a harmonious, "Aye."

Mrs. B. documented the motion and tallied the votes for the minutes.

Chuck took the unanimous endorsement as his cue to get up and leave. In one fell swoop, he gathered up his papers and headed to the door. Brandt was caught off-guard by his hasty exodus.

"Wait! Wait, Chuck! We have more to discuss." He rose up from his chair in an attempt to stop him from leaving.

"I'm done for the night!" he shouted over his shoulder. Chuck raced out the door before anyone could catch him.

Once again, Brandt leaned over for a quick puff from his inhaler. The man could only handle so much.

In a mellow tone, Jan said, "We've accomplished quite a bit this evening." The woman had an ethereal, calming effect. "Perhaps Desiree could have the Evites sent out by Wednesday morning?"

Larry made a note on his paper.

"Piper," Jan continued. "Why don't you and Carolyn take care of the décor? Brandt and I will pair to coordinate the auction items and paintings."

Piper scrunched up her nose in distaste, but chose not to disagree. Carolyn bowed her head to avoid making direct eye contact with anyone. Twice she'd been put in her place.

The next ten minutes were spent divvying up miscellaneous tasks. Reverend Black insisted on being the emcee of the event. When challenged by Larry for the job, he quickly pointed out the impressive numbers of his devoted flock as testament to his ability to please a crowd. Brandt proposed to reconvene on Wednesday evening in an effort to move things along. The others guffawed at the suggestion, leaving Brandt to capitulate by offering a follow-up email instead. The group firmly endorsed that suggestion.

The trustees dashed out of the conference room like prisoners being released from their cells, except for Piper and Brandt. She lingered behind collecting the nameplates, white pads, and empty water bottles alongside Mrs. B. without saying a word, a simple gesture of kindness for the executive assistant's earlier support. Brandt assisted Larry by putting away the microphone and recording system. The four of them worked in silence. As soon as the menial tasks were completed, Mrs. B. and Larry excused themselves to her cubicle. She had left some documents on her desk concerning some unfortunate patrons being banned from the library due to illicit behaviors. Brandt had already signed and dated the letters, so his presence was not needed. Left alone with Brandt, Piper cornered the nervous nelly concerning a pressing issue.

"Brandt, do you have a few minutes? I'd like to continue our conversation about the supposed misplacement of funds with the Library Friends group here at the Woodlawn branch. Larry didn't mention it at our meeting. Is there a reason why?" Piper positioned herself between Brandt and the door in a concerted effort to prevent him from making a speedy exit.

Like water dripping from a faucet, Brandt's sweat glands began to leak. The tiny beads of perspiration moistened his face making it difficult for him to concentrate. Piper took a decisive step forward violating the unwritten rule of adhering to an acceptable distance in terms of personal space. In a flash, his inhaler was drawn and puffed. Piper made no move towards backing up. Her intentions were unashamedly clear.

"I have nothing to report on the matter. Larry assured me he would take care of it." Brandt stood riveted to the spot in deference to Piper's wishes. He wiped off his face with a crumpled white handkerchief retrieved from his back pants pocket. He then lowered his eyes in an attempt to evade her piercing stare.

Piper cocked her head to the side. "And, you find his response acceptable? How so? He can't even take care of the multiple maintenance issues both Mrs. B. and Mrs. Johnson brought to his attention last month. " She proffered Brandt a little leeway as she seated herself in a grey, metal folding chair lined up against the wall.

Brandt drew in a noticeable breath of air. "Larry spoke with the president of the Friends group. Her name is Nancy something. I can't recall her last name right now. Supposedly, they're childhood friends or something like that. Anyway," he gestured with his left hand, "this Nancy person is actively investigating the whereabouts of all the proceeds from the used book sales and fundraisers for this fiscal year. She told him it might take a while, though."

"Why?" Piper crossed her arms across her chest.

"Many volunteers are gainfully employed. It's rather difficult to get a hold of them during business hours. Oftentimes, they only provide us with their home phone numbers because most prefer not to be bothered at work. Rest assured, Larry feels 100% confident Nancy will be able to sort things out in due time. I volunteered to make some calls, but he insisted on clearing up this slight monetary discrepancy, as he calls it, without my help."

Piper stood back up. "So, let me get this straight, Brandt. Nancy so-and-so has no idea where the money is? Really? How can that be in this day and age of technology where everything is saved, backed up, and stored on those little miniatures drives? I have a cute one that looks exactly like a tube of lipstick, by the way. Très chic. Anyway, must I remind you? We have strict policies concerning how funds and various donations are to be handled. The auditors are not going to be happy." She planted her hands on her hips in an act of defiance.

Brandt edged himself towards the exit. "Piper, why don't you concentrate on making the gala a huge success since it was your idea after all. I'll touch base with Larry in the morning and see what I can find out." He patted her on the shoulder.

"Although on second thought," he scratched his chin, "Larry seemed adamant about me butting out. Maybe I should give him some time to sort things out on his own. Our group is quick to criticize his administrative capabilities. Honestly, there's no need for us to quibble over this trivial matter. He'll figure it out sooner or later."

Piper leaned past him and snatched up her designer purse and brown leather trustee binder from the table. "Since when is $10,000 just a trivial matter, Brandt? I could buy plenty of Lilly Pulitzer shoes, scarves, and clothes with that amount of money, plus have a little extra left over for incidentals like a sparkly diamond bracelet for goodness sakes. What's wrong with you? I suggest you get your act together and figure out what's really going on around here. Remember, your name is at the top of the letterhead, not Larry's. For all you know, this could be just the tip of the iceberg." She hiked her purse up on her shoulder and hugged the leather folder tightly to her chest.

"Aren't you being a tad bit cynical, Piper?" he rolled his eyes. "We live in Woodlawn, Ohio, not New York City or L.A. I highly doubt there's a money laundering scam happening in our library system." He flipped off the light switch as Piper brushed past him on their way out of the building.

"Say what you will, Brandt, but I think you're being played for a fool." She patted him on the back, and grinned.

Brandt laughed off her comment as innocuous; however, his pensive look betrayed his worried thoughts. Brandt was on the verge of completing a ten year stint on the board. The last thing he needed was some newsworthy scandal involving the misappropriation of funds to tarnish his stellar reputation. Both he and Piper headed to their respective cars, each silently analyzing the precarious legal situation the board could potentially face.

Chapter 2
Changes to the Agenda

It took Piper less than five minutes to arrive home from the library. Parked on the left side of her driveway was a familiar black pick-up truck with its windows rolled down. Numerous bags of reddish-brown mulch accompanied by potted hydrangea plants were arbitrarily strewn about in the extra-long truck bed. There was only one man who would willingly submit himself to unsolicited manual labor…Rusty O'Brien. The strappingly handsome liquor store owner, turned part-time landscaper, wasn't just some ordinary red-haired oaf. Rather, he was an unabashedly suave expert when it came to love and romance. His blatant yet ingenious idea to surprise Piper with some free landscaping services in return for a late night romp was the reason these two lovebirds were in the midst of making plans to tie the knot. Great minds think alike.

Piper clicked the garage door opener attached to the driver's side visor with her neatly manicured finger. Her sleek, black Mercedes idled patiently while waiting for the white door to open. Using her time wisely, she unfastened the top two buttons of her blouse and adjusted her cleavage. In the center console, she found some bronzer in a gold compact along with a designer black make-up brush. Quickly, she swiped her face with a fresh dusting of sunshine. She continued to scrounge around in the side door compartments in search of random beauty products. "Score!" she shouted. Piper opened a brand new tube of Nars lipstick with joyful glee. With two purposeful strokes, her lips were painted in a bold pink hue, brightening her tired face. Glancing into the rearview mirror, Piper smiled at the hot, sexy look she had successfully created.

Piper eased the luxury mobile into the three-car garage. The distinct markings on the gray concrete floor guided her right into position. Her late husband Charles had painted the lines himself as warranted by the numerous scrapes on the passenger's side front panel. Piper turned off the engine and removed the key from the ignition. Leaning to her right, she snatched up her possessions from the unoccupied black leather seat and proceeded to exit the vehicle. With her belongings firmly pressed up against her chest, the giddy blonde bent over, tossing her golden mane forward and then back. Her perfectly highlighted hair cascaded into position, framing her heart-shaped face. Piper puckered her moist lips in preparation for what lay ahead. The sound of her heels clicking on the cement reverberated loudly, announcing her arrival to anyone in near proximity. A quick tap to the control panel mounted on the wall closed the immense garage door. With her one free hand on the doorknob, she pushed the door open only to be met by a half-naked, red-headed god standing directly on the other side. Two crystal goblets of red wine welcomed her home.

"Hey, babe." He propped the door open with his bare foot and motioned her to come inside.

Piper couldn't help but smile. "What are you doing here? I thought you'd still be in Cincinnati finishing up that commercial landscaping job you landed." She leaned over and planted a kiss on his lips.

"It's all done. Jim Wagner called me this morning and said he could lend me a hand. Business is slow. Said he could use the extra cash." He stepped aside so she could get by.

Piper walked into the kitchen and plopped her stuff on the counter. Rusty came up from behind and handed her a glass. An assortment of cheeses, dried fruits, and crackers were scattered about on an ordinary paper plate in the middle of the island. Piper chose a dried apricot from among the variety of fruits and popped it into her mouth. Savoring a generous sip of wine, she complimented Rusty on its fruity taste. She then said, "You know I'm not Jim's biggest fan. However, I do feel sorry for him. Laura took him to the cleaners when she filed for divorce. The guy was left with barely the shirt on his back. Speaking of shirts, where'd you leave yours?"

Rusty took this as a green light to set the night in motion. He maneuvered himself into position by pinning Piper up against the refrigerator door. "I thought you'd never ask." He moved her shirt aside and lightly kissed her toned shoulder. His tongue lingered for a brief second before their intimate moment was abruptly interrupted by the high-pitched sound of the smoke alarm.

Piper nearly doused Rusty with her wine trying to break free. The contents of her glass sloshed all over the pristine white tile floor as her arms flailed about in horror. Her reaction was par for the course. It was no secret. Her fire safety record left a lot to be desired. "What the heck is burning?" She frantically searched for the source.

"Damn!" Rusty threw his hands up in the air. "The tuna melts!" In one fell swoop, he grabbed a red-checked potholder off the countertop and flung open the stainless steel oven door. A billowing cloud of smoke escaped, causing the detectors to up their game. Rusty lurched backwards to avoid the fumes. Meanwhile Piper snatched Rusty's t-shirt off the countertop and proceeded to vigorously wave it in the air to dissipate the smoke. The ringing of the house phone only added to the cacophony of noise.

"Answer that! I'll take care of this!" he pointed in opposite directions. Rusty shoved her out of harm's way with his foot while teetering on the other—all the while, removing the baking sheet affixed with charred tuna melts from the stove.

Piper stumbled over to her desk and grabbed the cordless receiver. "Hello?" she yelled.

"I'm not hard of hearing, sis. Listen, I was thinking about the library ball or gala. Whatever you're calling it. What if Jim and I..." Penelope Davenport said.

"I don't have time for this now!" Used to being interrupted by her bossy older sister, Penelope took no issue with Piper's sharp tone. The tall, slender blonde, a pale version of Piper, was no stranger to her sister's range of emotional outbursts. Penelope worked part-time at the local dermatologist's office and was privy to much salacious gossip. She was all too happy to share this information with Piper during their frequent chats throughout each day. "Things are really heating up around here," Piper panted as she fanned herself with an old magazine found on her desk. The call waiting beeped in.

"Let me guess," Penelope chided. "Rusty is there. You two are worse than a bunch of hormonal teenagers. Just let me finish what I was saying. I know *you* think Jim is a complete moron, but *I* think everyone deserves a second chance especially since..."

Piper had no choice but to cut her off again. "Penelope, I have to take that call. It's 911!" she wailed. The emotional stress of the board meeting coupled with the havoc in the kitchen left no time or energy for Piper to explain. "I'll call you back. Promise."

Twenty minutes later, Piper and Rusty were peacefully lounging on the back deck nibbling on Chex mix and gluten-free cookies. Piper hadn't bothered to change out of her fancy pink suit. As for Rusty, he threw his t-shirt back on despite its smoky scent. All the windows on the first floor were wide-open, allowing the crisp, night air to seep into the house. The smoky vapors were long gone. Piper was able to convince both the alarm company and emergency services that, indeed, all was well in the O'Donnell household despite their initial reluctance to take her word for it. Who could blame them? Just a year ago she'd accidentally sent a building up in smoke.

"These cookies aren't half bad." Rusty popped a morsel in his mouth. "I had no idea you're allergic to gluten, babe. Good to know." He smiled at his fiancée.

Piper replied, "What are you talking about? I'm not allergic to gluten."

Rusty gave her a puzzling look. "Then why are we eating gluten-free cookies?" He grabbed the package and pointed to the verbiage.

She rolled her eyes. "I bumped into Jan, my hippie cohort on the library board, at CVS when I dropped off my prescription. Remember? I told you all about her. She's the quote "peace-loving woman" who in my opinion stirs up all the trouble. She has the rest of the board tricked into thinking she's all flowers and peace signs. Not me." Piper pounded her chest. "I see right through her. And, I'm not afraid to confront her when need be. I think if it were up to her, she'd fire Larry in a heartbeat. His scatter-brained ideas and flat-out incompetency exasperate her."

He nodded still concentrating on the list of ingredients.

"Back to the cookies. Jan highly recommended them. I figured it was some new type of health food fad, so I bought them. What do I know? I'm not what you'd call a nature girl." Piper insisted. She wiggled out of her high heels and tossed them aside.

"Really?" Rusty teased.

"Stop it! Listen to my story. These cookies were on sale two for five dollars, so I figured why not try them. I wanted to see what all the fuss was about." Piper stole one from the package and took a bite. Within seconds, she gagged and spit it out in her napkin. "Yuck! Remind me to toss them once we get inside," she sniffled. Reaching into her sleeve, she took out a tissue and wiped her nose.

"Still not feeling well?" He leaned over and brushed some wispy pieces of blonde hair out of her eyes.

Piper coughed. "No. I definitely have a sinus infection. This pressure is killing me. Unfortunately, the pharmacy closed before I had a chance to pick up my antibiotic."

"You should have texted me. I could have gotten it for you," Rusty scolded her.

She took a deep breath and leaned back. "I thought you'd be in Cincy. No worries. I'll have time to get it tomorrow. First, I need to make a quick stop by The Cardinal Shoppe to confirm the orders for the fall line of Lilly Pulitzer and a couple other designers. Then I can leave. That shouldn't take but twenty minutes, tops. I've bookmarked the pages already. The customers will be absolutely blown away when they see the chic selections. The colors and textures are bold, yet classic." Piper's eyes sparkled with enthusiasm whenever she shared her fashion expertise.

Rusty said, "Sounds like you've got things under control. Liz Monroe hit the jackpot when she hired you on for her store, babe." He squeezed her arm.

A nearby bush rustled taking the couple by surprise. The two watched as Ralph Lauren magically appeared.

Piper's finicky feline shared a love-hate relationship with Rusty. The cat sniffed his shoes, turned up his nose, and vanished back into the night.

Piper continued, "I sent Liz a text during the board meeting to let her know of my plan. There is no way I can work my four-hour shift, not with this headache." She rubbed her temples for emphasis.

Last holiday season, the owner of the fanciful boutique turned out to be short-staffed. After some heartfelt persuasion, Liz convinced Piper to leave behind her part-time bookkeeping position at Peeps & Petals for a career better suited to her "God-given" talents. As Liz so eloquently pointed out, Piper's desire to keep abreast of the latest styles and trends was reflected by her voguish attire. As a walking billboard for the shop, Liz couldn't think of anyone more qualified to take over as the store's primary buyer. With Liz's retirement years staring her straight in the face, the prospect of turning over the reins to a fashionista like Piper made perfect sense.

"So, Booklovers' Ball: Art & Sold. I like it. Very creative, Piper." Rusty took a swig of water. Beads of perspiration adhered to his upper lip. "It's awfully sticky out here. Want to call it a night?" He began to gather up the bowls of snacks.

Piper patted his hand. "Not just yet." She gently removed them from his grasp and placed them back on the side table. "I want to talk with you about something." A serious look crossed her face. Rusty fidgeted in his lounge chair as he ran his fingers through his hair.

"How would you feel about Penelope and Jim going to the ball together?" Piper asked.

Rusty sighed with relief. "That's what you wanted to talk about?" He grabbed the bowls and stood up. "What do I care? Jim Wagner is a single guy now. He can date whomever he pleases. He doesn't need permission from me to date your sister. We're all good now that Laura is out of the picture. The question is how do you feel?"

Piper scrambled trying to get up. "I'm totally fine with it. If you ask me, his laundry list of issues stemmed from his ex-wife, Laura. With her gone, I think we're going to see a new and improved Jim Wagner. Plus, my sister is bored with Dr. King. That man is a player. Too bad he's also her boss. Penelope is looking for someone more stable. I will tell her it's a go first thing in the morning. Speaking of family, how are the renovations going at your mother's house? Did Jim say anything? I can only imagine the stress he's under having to deal with Helen and Capt. Morgan on a daily basis. No wonder he offered to help you with the job in Cincy. God bless him. I hope you paid him double what he earned." Both Piper and Rusty made a point of staying clear of the chaos ensuing at the Morgan homestead. The two agreed it was in the best interests of everyone involved. "The house desperately needed to be refurbished, though. It will be much more handicap-accessible for her once Jim installs all of the upgrades. She will be pleased."

The two entered the house and worked side by side to clean up the kitchen. The gluten-free cookies were slipped right into the trash can followed by the leftover appetizers.

"The next thing on my agenda is to convince your mom to let me decorate it. I'm envisioning something a little more contemporary with clean lines. No more overstuffed sofas emblazoned in corduroy. And bright yellow is not an option for the walls. Come to think of it, when I'm feeling better, I'll swing by Chuck's hardware store and pick up some sample tins of the new Jeff Lewis paint line. You know, Chuck's hip wife is the brains behind that business. She keeps him in the loop of the latest trends and colors. Yes, indeed, grays and neutrals are in your mother's future."

"That might take some convincing on your part," Rusty added.

Piper grabbed Rusty's chin in a playful manner. "Lest you forget. If it weren't for me, their wedding reception would have been some ordinary affair." She leaned in and kissed him squarely on his lips.

"Mmm hmm," he moaned in agreement.

Memories of the union flooded Piper's mind. Helen tied the knot with the cantankerous policeman in a private ceremony at the courthouse last December. The celebration included the who's who of Woodlawn. In a nod of appreciation for his fellow first responders, the local firehouse was selected as the site of their reception. The prerequisite red and white streamers hanging from the trucks were replaced with exquisite poinsettias and glittering snowflakes adorning the station from the rafters. The winter wonderland was the talk of the town, thanks to Piper's resourcefulness and intuitive decorator's touch.

"I think I'm going to call it a night," Rusty offered. Tucking his hands into his jeans pockets, he took a step back from her.

Piper closed the gap and pushed at his stomach. "Afraid of my germs?"

He smirked. "Yep. Something like that." His penetrating green eyes dared her to come closer.

Piper scolded him with her finger. "You should have thought about that before you went all in, Romeo. Your tongue down my throat…not so smart."

Rusty swallowed hard.

Her giddy outburst of laughter broke the tension.

Rusty grabbed her hands and pulled her into a tight embrace. "Get some sleep. I'll call first thing in the morning to check on you. Promise." A light kiss planted on the top of Piper's head ended the lovers' eventful night.

Left alone in a darkened house, Piper made her way up the staircase using the light of her iPhone to lead the way. Her tired body writhed in pain as she staggered up the steps. Half-way there, the sound of an incoming text startled her. She propped herself up against the bannister welcoming the slight reprieve. It took but a second for her to retrieve the message. Piper moaned in frustration. Her least favorite person, Carolyn, of course, wanted to meet at ten in the morning to discuss the details for the ball. Despite wanting to blow her off, Piper texted back *yes*. She figured there was no use putting off the inevitable. Step by step, she continued the formidable climb to the top. Her drained body faltered at the sight of the threshold to her long-awaited bedroom. As she meandered towards her private sanctuary, a trail of discarded clothes marked her path. The moment her aching head touched the luxurious silk pillowcase, Piper closed her eyes praying for a night of restful sleep.

Chapter 3
Recognitions

The howling winds and thundering rain outside her second floor bedroom window mirrored the aches and pains resonating throughout Piper's body. Morning arrived without her garnering a wink of sleep. A near-miss tumble upon a pile of strewn clothes on the plush carpeted floor sent expletives spluttering from her mouth. Not the usual ladylike demeanor for such a classy lady like Piper. A piercing headache coupled with crappy weather dampened her normal positive chi. The very thought of having to meet Carolyn later that morning made her even crankier. Piper grabbed the first clean outfit she could find, cream-colored designer pants and a blush-toned blouson. Topping it off with her favorite pink fedora, she was able to hide the rat's nest on her head. Some chunky jewels from BaubleBar.com and her favorite LOVE inscribed rose-colored signature ring completed her harried look. Bare minimal makeup and a perfunctory brushing of her pearly white teeth sent her on the way.

First on the agenda was a quick trip to The Cardinal Shoppe to take care of business. Per usual, she dashed by her favorite Starbuck's drive-thru for a skinny vanilla latte to fuel up. At the rate she was going, Piper would need more than a jolt of caffeine to get through her day. As luck would have it, her favorite cashier was working the window. A few minutes of frivolous banter brought a smile to Piper's pale face. After a swipe of her credit card, she was back en route sipping coffee while listening to pop music on satellite radio. From the corner of her eye, she spotted a woman in a blue SUV in her rearview mirror following way too close for comfort. A slight tap of her breaks sent the menacing vehicle swerving into the oncoming lane of traffic nearly missing a white van. The blaring of horns rattled Piper's nerves, which caused her to slosh piping hot coffee on her pants. Her knee-jerk reaction to pull over to the curb was mimicked by the driver of the SUV.

After slamming the car into park, Piper leaned over to rummage through the center console. Underneath a mound of beauty products, she found a red canister of wet wipes. Pulling out a handful of dampened sheets, she got to work. The right leg of her buff pants was sopping wet, stained with brown speckles of coffee. Vehemently scrubbing the spatters, she attempted to save the fabric from further damage. She mumbled some choice words under her breath while checking her rearview mirror as to the whereabouts of the driver of the SUV. Her efforts were cut short by the rat-a-tat-tat on her driver's side window. Piper twisted around to find Desiree Hamilton with her face pushed up against the glass. Similar to a doggie in a window, the young woman panted in anticipation of chatting it up with her friend. Sadly for her, that was not the case. Piper's snarling face signaled the need for Desiree to take a few steps back.

Biting her lip, Desiree waved hello. She followed up with, "Hey, Piper! It's me." Attired in form-fitting yoga wear, the twenty-something looked as if she weighed maybe ninety pounds soaking wet. Her noticeably perky breasts guaranteed a first in show for any wet t-shirt contest she desired to enter.

Piper tapped the button for the automatic window. The two women watched in silence as the barrier between them lowered.

Piper was the first to speak. "Mind if I ask…what the heck were you thinking following me so closely like that? You almost caused an accident!" Her Barbie-doll face was scrunched up with tell-tale signs of distress. She chucked the used wad of wipes onto the dashboard.

Desiree smacked on her chewing gum and then twisted a strand of brown hair with her finger. "Um, I need to talk with you. Sooner rather than later. Seemed like the perfect opportunity." She glanced around as if looking for someone.

"You could've just called me!" Piper's hands flailed in the air. "Or even a text would have worked better than riding my bumper." Piper took a moment to size up her colleague while drawing in some deep, calming breaths. In contrast, the skittish IT tech teetered from side-to-side, nibbled on her nails, and then peered over her petite shoulder. The ingénue clearly exhibited signs of jittery behavior. No yoga-inspired "om" for her. As if on cue, Piper took this as a signal to get herself back in check. No need to rattle Desiree's nerves any further. It was only spilled coffee. That's why God made dry cleaners and wet wipes.

The sound of cars approaching caused Desiree to inch in closer towards Piper's vehicle. With her back to the onrushing traffic, Desiree blew a gigantic bubble of gum mere inches from Piper's sickly face.

Piper's gnarly sinus infection played nasty tricks on her better judgment. A problem she'd come across on many occasions, sick or well. The verdict was not in her favor this time. One swift poke from the tip of her fingernail caused the bubble to burst all over Desiree's face. "Oh, my word! I am so sorry! My hand slipped. Really, it did." Their chance meeting was heading from bad to worse. Taunting the girl didn't bode well for her desired results.

Clawing the gum off of her face, Desiree replied, "No worries. Accidents happen."

"Especially with you at the wheel, right?" Piper's attempt to make light of the situation failed. Like a train running on a crooked track, she was getting nowhere fast.

Desiree mustered on despite the uncomfortable situation. "I have some library scoop for you." She lifted her eyebrows in an attempt to lure Piper in. No surprise, Piper willingly obliged.

Tapping Desiree on the arm with her well-manicured hand Piper said, "Why don't you come in here on the passenger's side where it is nice and cozy?" She patted the black leather seat next to her with the opposite hand. "I don't want you to get hit by those passing cars. Idiot drivers!" A quick swipe of her belongings cleared the space next to her. She heaved everything into the back seat. Piper then leaned over and pushed open the heavy door for her gossipmonger friend.

Within seconds, Desiree jogged around the car and slipped inside. First thing she did was check her smartphone for messages.

"Anything of interest?" Piper greeted her with a warm smile.

Desiree ignored her question. "I don't have much time. My yoga class starts in fifteen minutes. I don't want to lose my spot."

"I can see you need the exercise." Piper's attempt at good behavior was short-lived. She pinched herself as punishment. It was hard to be sympathetic towards a skinny rail devoted to fitness. It wasn't too long ago Piper fit that bill. These days, not so much. Piper sucked in her slight muffin top and covered it with her blousy pink-striped shirt.

Once again, Desiree brushed over the comment. She grabbed hold of her brown hair and twisted away. "I figured if anyone on the library board would be interested in a dose of drama it would be you. This cockamamie story is right up your alley." Touché. The zinger was well deserved.

"Keep talking." Piper flicked her cell phone on silent and sat upright.

A frantic glance at her watch indicated Desiree's time to be limited. "I never repeat gossip, so please listen carefully."

The irony of her statement was not lost on Piper. She instinctively raised her eyebrows in anticipation.

"The day of the board meeting, I cut out early. Let's just say I had a re-check with my…um…surgeon late in the afternoon." Desiree adjusted her taut bra strap.

"Go on," Piper urged the young woman. A quick once over confirmed Piper's initial observation. The young woman's boobs were undeniably silicone-filled.

Desiree continued, "Larry has me working after library hours on this special computer project to track the sales and profits from the Library Friends group. I'm not really supposed to be talking about it because it's some big secret. Larry says he wants me to work out all the kinks before he unveils it to the whole board."

Piper's brain started churning. She knew darn well there was some discrepancy with the funds. She'd heard it straight from Brandt's mouth. According to Larry, he was working with Nancy to pinpoint the whereabouts of the monies. "Does Brandt know Larry is spearheading this special assignment?"

Desiree started fiddling with her hair again. "Funny you should ask. When I swung back by the branch to pick up my notes, I walked in on Larry and Brandt in a heated discussion."

"Discussion or argument? There's a difference," Piper clarified. She positioned herself a bit closer to Desiree.

Desiree lowered her head, picking imaginary lint from her black pants as she continued. "Argument, then. I was annoyed to have to return to the library at such an ungodly hour anyway. Larry seems to think I have no life. He's constantly texting me about absurd questions that can wait until the next business day. And when we're working together, he invades my personal space. Not on purpose. It's just a habit. I probably could sue him for sexual harassment, you know. Not to mention, his leering eyes give me the creeps." Her face tensed up. "But anyway, Brandt was trying to put the kibosh on Larry's plans to handle his so-called private investigation concerning the funds. He was threatening to expose Larry to the board as being the responsible party for the mismanagement issue."

Piper's wide-eyed expression matched her amazement in what Desiree was spewing. "How can that be? Does Brandt have any proof?"

Desiree perked up. "Here's the thing. It's no secret Larry has criticized Brandt's leadership initiatives publicly on numerous occasions, and has aimed barbs at his sexual orientation as well. Why he's so uncomfortable with Brandt having a man for a partner is beyond me in this day and age. His not-so-subtle innuendos have been duly noted by the other board members. He's even been reprimanded by Reverend Black for his insensitivity. Could be he's using that as a way to undermine Brandt and get all the power for himself. Who knows what goes on in that oddball's brain! Truthfully, I'm surprised this is news to you, Piper. I thought you were in the know." Desiree furrowed her brow. "Hmm, anyway, whether he has proof or not, Brandt has an axe to grind with Mr. so-called Library Director and vice versa. The two would do just about anything to take each other down. I know that for a fact. I've worked closely with both of them. Too closely!" She reiterated.

It was Piper's turn to fidget in her seat. Her thought process was on overload. From the homophobic references to Desiree's admission that Larry's behavior crossed the line, she didn't know where to start. More importantly, why did Desiree feel the need to let her in on this secret? Unless Desiree had her own agenda. Piper needed to get to the bottom of this. If only her throbbing headache weren't such a distraction.

"So what do you want from me?" Piper laid it all out there.

Throwing her shoulders back, Desiree demanded, "Help me get rid of Larry."

Piper's bewildered expression revealed her utter disbelief. "And, why would I want to do that? Granted, I think Larry is an idiot with a big head and an ego to match. Narrow-minded, indeed. But, it's not my place to decide who stays and who goes. I'm a newbie on the board. I need to prove my worth, not get involved in matters that don't concern me. I think it's best if you let these two men work out their own issues without interference."

The pucker on Desiree's face was far from becoming. "But, what about the missing funds?" She tried to goad her into submission.

Piper relented, "That, my friend is something worth investigating. Was anyone else present when they had their clandestine tête-à-tête?"

Without missing a beat she said, "You mean besides Carolyn?" A devilish smirk accompanied Desiree's response.

Piper noticed a sudden shift in her so-called friend's demeanor. Desiree was no longer a timid bystander.

No, she mimicked a Cheshire cat waiting to pounce on her unsuspecting victim. With a simple question, Desiree had raised the stakes. Yet, she misjudged Piper's response. Piper fully recognized what this calculating young woman was up to and she wanted no part of it. Piper was too smart to allow Desiree to pigeonhole her as the instigator. "Perhaps you best speak with her then. Carolyn is better schooled in dealing with sensitive issues such as this one." Piper cocked her head to one side and then leaned in closer. "Yes, she would be your go-to person, not me." To drive her point home, Piper picked up the key fob and unlocked the car. "Time for yoga." She smiled.

Desiree's stunned look betrayed her disappointment. She twitched her lips, bit her thumb nail, and chirped goodbye. Desiree couldn't get out of Piper's car fast enough. Less than thirty seconds later, the blue SUV disappeared from sight.

Piper instantly grabbed her cell phone. A quick call to vent to her fiancé Rusty was in order. Luckily, he picked up on the first ring. After filling him in on the bizarre encounter, Rusty concurred with her initial thoughts. Piper and Desiree's supposed accidental meeting was completely premeditated. Piper pointed out to him Desiree's reputation for being nothing less than brilliant, citing Larry's very public praises as her proof. Before she could go any further, Rusty interrupted her chatter with a reminder of the pressing time. If she was going to make the meeting with Carolyn, she had to get moving. The couple made plans to touch base after Piper's rendezvous.

A furtive glance at her Michael Kors rose gold wristwatch dictated the need to floor the gas pedal. Piper's sleek Mercedes zipped along Route 924 to The Cardinal Shoppe in record time. Business had to come first. The owner, Liz, depended on her.

The parking lot was vacant save a stray cat trying earnestly to catch a Monarch butterfly. Piper's sigh of relief calmed her psyche as she pulled into her preferred spot right in front of the shop. She'd be able to tend to business without interruptions. The store would be buzzing in about an hour or two depending on what celebrity was booked on *Live with Kelly & Michael*. Oftentimes, Piper set her work schedule around its guest line-up. An appearance by the newly married George Clooney guaranteed a bonus half hour for busywork like folding clothes or rearranging the merchandise. The news of his engagement had sent waves of disappointed women to Rusty's liquor store. It was amazing how such newsworthy announcements in the entertainment world dictated activity in a small town like Woodlawn.

By the time Piper sat down at her desk, the clock chimed nine o'clock. She took off her hat and tossed it on the counter. A quick fluffing of her straggly hair kept her occupied as she waited for the computer to warm up. A perfunctory glance around the quaint shop set her mind at ease. Whoever closed last night left the place in tip-top shape. *One less thing for me to do,* she thought.

Within fifteen minutes she had submitted the fall orders. Only two of the items on her list were on backorder. She was especially pleased with the jewelry pieces she ordered from Alex and Ani. This lifestyle brand was a bit avant-garde for The Cardinal Shoppe's clientele, yet their ideas about empowering communities by encouraging sustainability was exactly the message Piper was looking for in her fashion choices. This year, she decided to scale back on the Tory Burch line. Despite being a fan favorite and one of Piper's personal go-to designers, the ladies in town were inundated with the signature T's on their shoes, handbags, and jewelry. Time to find another designer to add to the store for a fresh look. Stella McCartney was too pricey for her patrons. Maybe some Kate Spade or Trina Turk. Piper was still debating.

With her work completed, Piper grabbed a yellow sticky note from a nearby cube and scratched a note to Liz letting her know the orders were placed. The roaring of Katy Perry's voice interrupted her mid-sentence. Checking the caller ID, she recognized the familiar number. "Hey, Neil. I'm on my way. I received the automated call that my prescription was ready."

"Hello, Piper. How are you today? Nice weather we're having. It's refreshing to see the green grass and flower buds." A stickler for formalities, the pharmacist took joy in conversing with Piper. Whenever she was in the store, he made sure to wait on her himself. An aging has-been, he was stuck in a 1950s time warp of gentile behavior.

"Not really up for the pleasantries, Neil. My apologies. This sinus infection has zapped all the good manners out of my brain. Please tell me there's not a problem with my prescription. I'm dying." Piper took one last look at the store before setting the alarm. By the time Neil responded, she was already sitting in her car with the engine revving.

Neil's calm voice oozed through the phone. "Oh, yes, Piper, the prescription is here waiting for you. You know the missus always says...."

Poor Neil was cut off mid-sentence by Piper's alleged bad connection. An excuse would be rendered after she had the antibiotics in hand. For now, her main objective was to swing by the pharmacy and then make it to the club by ten o'clock for her meeting with Carolyn.

The neighborhood pharmacy was located not far from the diner. Situated on a busy corner on Main

Street, it was the only drugstore in town. The parking lot gods were with her, as Piper spied yet another vacant spot right in front. She took a quick look in both directions before exiting her car in hopes of avoiding any familiar faces. With the sidewalk cleared, she scooted right into the store.

The pharmacy counter was located in the far back corner of the store past the magazines and make-up aisle. Piper gave in to temptation and snatched a tube of Maybelline mascara and some pink lip gloss along the way. Imagine her disappointment when she spotted the long line meandering down the laxative aisle. With no choice but to join the other waiting customers, she queued up behind a familiar looking man. One quick glance at his shoes and Piper couldn't believe her good fortune.

"Well, hello, Larry," she whispered in his left ear despite his aversion towards her. Larry had made it very clear from the get-go that he had objected to Piper serving as a member of the library board of trustees. At one of her very first meetings he'd told her so, in supposed confidence, although his loud voice carried throughout the room. Sure, Piper didn't have business acumen like many of the others, nor was she independently wealthy. Neither of these was his bone of contention. Rather, her cosmopolitan views coupled with her ability to see right through his phony persona made her an imminent threat to Larry's success. His distaste for her popularity with Judge Halbreath poured salt into his already deep wound. Yes, Larry recognized Piper for exactly what she was...a threat, an ardent competitor, and most importantly a woman he could not trust.

His comb-over smacked Piper directly in the face, a mishap resulting from their close proximity. The frown on his face did little to mask his displeasure of finding

Piper breathing down his neck. "Hello, Piper. I presume you're not feeling well, or is this some sort of new style you're sporting." He eyed her up and down. "Not your best look," he whispered back into her ear.

Piper stuck with her agenda and ignored his anticipated snarky remark. She played the sympathy card instead. "I have the worst sinus infection." She draped her hand across her forehead. "Pardon me for my behavior at the meeting on Monday night. I could feel something coming on." Piper began to toy with her purse. Grabbing a tissue from a side pocket, she daintily blew her nose for the full effect.

The line of customers started to dwindle causing the pair to advance closer to the counter. It became apparent the majority of folks were dropping off prescriptions rather than picking up. The top of Neil's head could now be seen bobbing up and down behind the row of computer screens as he moved back and forth along the counter.

In an obvious attempt to prevent Piper from invading his personal space, Larry folded his arms across his chest and took two more steps forward. "I accept your apology. If truth be told, I thought you were being a bossypants. Pushy even. As a new addition to the board, it's best to take your cues from the more seasoned members." His disparaging comments complemented the smug look on his face.

Piper squinted from the one eye that felt mediocre at best. "I'm surprised you misinterpreted my actions as being pushy or perhaps even bullying for that matter. I want what's best for the library. That includes tightening our purse strings. We need to keep a watchful eye on our expenses and income. Speaking of which, have you spoken to Brandt lately?"

All of a sudden Larry broke into an uncontrollable coughing fit causing Neil to dart out from behind the counter to see who was causing such a commotion.

"Larry! Piper! My two favorite customers." Not skipping a beat, he moved Piper out of harm's way. The poor library director found himself bent over at the knees gasping for breath with his signature fold of hair unhinged from his balding head. With a quick jerk, Neil had him upright and on display to the line of bystanders. Speaking directly to Larry in a quiet voice he said, "Let me go ahead and help Piper while you catch your breath."

Neil took his time conferring with Piper about the possible contraindications before dispensing the meds. Piper nodded and smiled during the process with her mind clearly elsewhere. He managed to squeeze in a quick story about his grandkids, oblivious to Piper's tuning him out, before the grumbling of waiting customers prompted him to move on.

As Piper was leaving, she mentioned to Larry her impending meeting with Carolyn at the club. He surprised her by suggesting a quick stop by the library to pick up the latest budget numbers to help with their planning. He informed her that the report could be found in his office on the left side of his desk. He even went so far as to suggest she just help herself. The door remained unlocked, just as he had left it.

"Desiree compiled the information late last night," he said while pulling his brown wallet from the back pocket of his tan khakis.

Piper thanked him for being so accommodating and left the store with a skip in her step. The last thing she'd expected was Larry's help. Having a leg up on Carolyn warmed her cheeks.

Backtracking to the library added more minutes to Piper's already tight timeframe. The polite thing to do would have been to call Carolyn to let her know she might be running late, but that didn't happen. Piper opted to chance it instead. Upon her arrival, she was met with a parking lot full of cars. Piper let out a screech contemplating what to do next. Just as she was maneuvering her signature double-park doozy behind a red minivan, a spot opened up. Within seconds, she was scooting through the sliding glass doors, averting her eyes from the front desk. The last thing she needed was a menacing stare from a nosy librarian concerning her swift entrance.

Larry's office was located in the rear of the building with a separate exit used only by him. He bragged that he could come and go as he pleased which irked some of the board members. Rumor had it Jan had proposed sealing the exit a couple years back solely for safety purposes, or so she'd claimed. The motion was denied by a slim margin, but her point was duly noted by the others. Larry's comings and goings were being monitored, not that it seemed to make much difference. His questionable behavior towards Desiree, case in point, left a lot to be desired. In the past, the director made his own rules whether his staff liked it or not. Now that Piper was on the board, Larry's safe haven was in constant jeopardy, or so she liked to think.

The library was busy for a Tuesday morning. The line of computer desks was filled with users. Piper whisked right by the patrons in an effort to make up for lost time. When she neared the long back hallway, she quickened her pace. Turning the bend, she spotted the brown wooden doorframe in the distance. As Piper approached the office, she noticed the door was slightly ajar. The shiny brass nameplate temporarily blinded her due to the bright sun reflecting off the showy placard. At that same moment, Piper felt a tingle down her back causing her to temporarily pause. She turned around to see if anyone was following her, but the hallway was vacant.

Mrs. B. was missing from her designated perch outside of Larry's office. Piper surmised a coffee or restroom break must have been in order. The clutter amassed on her standard-issue desk signaled a busy day ahead. Navigating around the unoccupied desk, she pushed her way right through the door in search of the documents. In retrospect, Piper should have known Larry's offer was too good to be true. Yes, the papers he'd promised sat neatly on the left corner of his desk right where he said they would be. But, what she found lying in a heap on the floor caused Piper to drop her beloved designer purse and faint.

Chapter 4
Approval of Minutes

Waking to the sound of distant voices was par for the course for Piper. Like any closet reality star wannabe, this thrilling sensation happened to be a common occurrence. Yet this time when she opened her eyes there were no paparazzi. No swarming hordes of adoring fans begging for autographs. Just a group of hovering bodies invading her personal space. A quick flitter of her eyelashes produced the same results. This was no fan club meeting.

"She's awake!" announced a familiar female voice. "She opened her eyes."

"It's about time," replied a grumpy male.

Piper debated whether to continue the impromptu snooze fest or acknowledge the presence of the curious onlookers. Either way, an interrogation seemed inevitable. Might as well get this over with as quickly as possible, she concluded. Three deep breaths and a peaceful moment of Zen gave her the courage to come back to life.

With the help of the benevolent Mrs. B., Piper sat upright. Adjacent to her willowy body rested a damp, white towel awaiting her use. Piper dabbed her moist forehead as she gathered her bearings, taking in a perfunctory glance at her present surroundings. Mrs. B. asserted her motherly self by pushing a small paper cup filled to the brim with clear liquid to Piper's lips. The frazzled blonde affirmed to her companion the cold water felt good as it trickled down her dry throat. A makeshift curtain separated the group from the rest of the limited office space. All eyes in the cramped room fixated on Piper's crumpled figure.

For once, Piper decided to adhere to her mother's sage childhood advice. This precarious situation called for being seen and not heard. The festering brood perched nearby presumed she would start babbling at any moment, as was the norm for her. But, not this time. Piper's eyes darted from face to face in search of answers, but came up empty-handed. Her plump, pink lips remained sealed shut. Her reluctance to chime in prompted the man in charge to initiate the conversation.

"Dare I ask what you're doing here, Piper?" the frumpy gentleman inquired. Dressed in a leather bomber jacket, plaid shirt, and jeans, he slowly adjusted his Cincinnati Reds baseball cap without making eye contact. It was as if he knew her answer would take a while. It was plain to see from his attire he paid no mind to the weatherman. The calendar might have read April, but his outfit screamed the dead of winter.

"Captain Morgan," Piper sighed. It didn't take being a rocket scientist for her to figure out that if Capt. Morgan were around, trouble ensued. To his left stood a cantankerous fifty-something policewoman with knotty hands firmly planted on her hips. To his right twitched some bald-headed, official-looking dude with bulging muscles holding a random clipboard. The scene caused Piper's stomach to churn. "What happened?" She rubbed her head for full effect.

As if on cue, the hanging white sheet separating the known from the unknown billowed to the floor. A puny corpse with an outstretched hand was pinned underneath a fallen bookcase. At first sight, Piper presumed the victim immobilized by the heavy wooden structure to be a female. Yet, upon closer inspection the worn brown loafers proved her initial guess incorrect.

Even the victim's hair and body were absconded from view. If it weren't for the sparkle from Mr. Muscles' gold LeBron James high tops catching her eye, Piper might have missed the tell-tale sign lingering not far from the victim's body. An errant inhaler rested peacefully on the industrial strength carpet.

A loud gasp escaped from Piper's mouth. "Oh, my word!"

Capt. Morgan leaned in closer to Piper's pale face and whispered, "Please tell me you had nothing to do with this."

Mrs. B. quickly came to Piper's defense, "Capt. Morgan! How could you even ask such a question?" She squeezed Piper right up against her generous bosom in a protective embrace.

The seasoned cop laughed at her naiveté and said, "Trust me. She's no innocent bystander."

Evidently, Mrs. B. thought otherwise. Her venomous stare aimed directly at the policeman's squirrely green eyes rebuked his preposterous statement. "Really? How would you know?"

Mr. Muscles lost patience with the trio's antics, giving the lady officer the go-ahead to begin shooing the clamorous entourage into the long hallway. Mrs. B. aptly held the crook of Piper's arm while judiciously directing the path of the feeble blonde's steps. Piper retrieved her ginormous purse from the floor before Mr. Muscles had a chance to tag it for evidence. Her beautifully manicured hand scrounged around the bottom of the designer bag in a desperate search for something important. Within seconds, a sparkly pink cell phone emerged from the abyss. Piper cleverly slipped it in her pants' pocket. As for Capt. Morgan, he trailed a few paces behind, making sure he was well within earshot of any significant dribbles of their stolen conversation.

As they emerged from the back hall, a host of people congregating near the circulation desk greeted them, including the feisty Mrs. Johnson, the librarian in charge. A uniformed policeman kept them at bay in order to give Piper and Mrs. B. ample space to skirt the locals. A few edged closer to the self-check-out kiosk for a better view only to be escorted directly out of the building by Mrs. Johnson. Piper and Mrs. B. were directed to the board conference room, which was serving as the holding area until Capt. Morgan was freed from his present duties. Upon entering, Piper collapsed into the worn, brown leathered upholstered chair situated at the head of the long table. The sound of her cell phone vibrating perked her right up, that is until she read the name of the caller. With a vigorous swipe across the screen with her manicured finger, she answered the call and then put it on speakerphone. Propping her feet up onto the adjacent chair, she prepared herself for the inevitable rant headed her way.

"Piper O'Donnell! You have some nerve! I waited over thirty minutes for you. I looked like a complete fool. How dare you skip our scheduled meeting without giving me the courtesy of a phone call or a text! That's downright rude and inconsiderate. You leave me no choice but to report your negligence to Brandt. I will recommend to him that you are removed from the planning committee effective immediately."

Without missing a beat, Piper volunteered, "Actually, Carolyn, I'm here with him now, but something tells me he doesn't care about your silly recommendation. He has more pressing issues at hand."

"Really? We'll see about that. Hand him your phone. I'd like to speak with him myself," Carolyn insisted.

"He's unable to come to the phone right now." Her voice mimicked a recorded message.

A barrage of unladylike words spewed from Carolyn's mouth, inciting Mrs. B. to join in on the conversation. "Hush, Carolyn! You sound like a babbling fool."

"Mrs. B.?" Carolyn asked. "Is that you?"

"You betcha! Pipe yourself down right this instant. Brandt could care less about your missed meeting." The old woman shook her head in disgust.

"And *why* do you think that?" Carolyn demanded.

Piper did not mince words. "He's dead."

"What do you mean *dead*?" Carolyn squealed.

A voice from the other side of the room hollered, "Hang up the phone!"

All eyes shifted to the intimidating figure planted firmly in the doorway.

"Hello? Hello? Is that Capt. Morgan I hear in the background?" Carolyn would not let up. "What's going on, Piper? What did you do now?"

With one nimble tap, Carolyn was robbed of an answer. For once, Piper was more than willing to oblige Capt. Morgan's request. However, the policeman's stern countenance did little to deter Piper from high-fiving Mrs. B. in a celebratory salute.

Capt. Morgan instructed the ladies to stay put for the time being since he had more pressing issues at hand. The ladies acquiesced by promising to remain sequestered from the patrons and nosy library staff until his prompt return. On his way out the door, he changed his mind and ordered Mr. Muscles to supervise in order to prevent any monkeyshines in his absence.

Meanwhile down the hall, his staff busied themselves sectioning off the crime scene with yellow police tape. The forensic photographers meticulously snapped photos of Larry's office in an effort to capture any and all evidence left behind. Following standard protocol, every inch of space was dusted for fingerprints while the tiny window behind the desk was checked for signs of forced entry. Evidence samples were gathered and tagged for future inspection. When Capt. Morgan felt assured by his staff that the area had been sufficiently searched and examined, he signaled for the coroner to proceed with his analysis of the body.

Capt. Morgan marched back down the hall to get Piper's take on the murder. Upon entering the room, he found Piper filing her nails and Mrs. B. taking a catnap in the corner. The clearing of his throat grabbed their attention.

"All done?" Piper asked.

"Not yet," he answered. "I have some questions for you."

He began by asking Piper to carefully retrace her steps that morning to the best of her knowledge, leading up to the discovery of Brandt's lifeless body. At certain points he paused to gently probe Piper for clarification of her somewhat disjointed thoughts. In true Piper fashion, she botched up his methodical procedure by adding her muddled views based purely on her warped perception of reality. Their conversation took a hasty nosedive when she digressed on the subject of Carolyn wanting to have passed canapés during the cocktail hour rather than the committee approved appetizer stations. Before Capt. Morgan knew what was happening, she had him signed up as chair of the ticket sales committee.

"Exactly when did you discover Brandt's body, Piper?" He tried to steer her back to the investigation.

"When I entered the room, silly! Now, do you think we should have tables of eight or ten for the gala? I see pluses and minuses for both, but I think I'm leaning towards ten. It's a nice round number. Your thoughts?" She wiggled her pursed lips from side to side.

The man nixed his attempted cross examination, seeing as he'd gathered not one iota of pertinent information from the gabby blonde. A perfunctory request for Piper not to leave town ended their futile conversation.

"Glad I could help." The fair-haired maven smiled. "Now if I were you, I'd start drumming up a list of suspects. If you need suggestions, you know where to find me." She grabbed her purse, hugged Mrs. B, and then exited the room.

As soon as Piper's feet hit the pavement, she was on the phone with Rusty talking a mile a minute. Her hand gestures flailed all over the place making her look like a crazy lunatic. Once inside her black car, she connected to Bluetooth and carried on the conversation all the way home.

"So, babe, who do you think is responsible for Brandt's murder? Did you take a mental picture of the crime scene?" Rusty couldn't help but get involved. His defunct private eye venture left him with a constant itch for anything investigative.

Piper guffawed with laughter. "I knew you were going to ask me that!" She pulled into the local drive-thru for her second jolt of caffeine for the morning. "I memorized every inch of what I could see. C'mon over to my place and I'll fill you in. Do you want anything from Starbuck's?"

"Please! The usual," he requested.

"One grande black coffee of the day coming right up!" she chimed. "See you soon."

The line of cars snaked around the building, filled with fellow caffeine addicts in search of a late afternoon pick-me-up. To pass the time, Piper took out her cell phone to check social media for the latest celebrity scoop. While gushing over a post by her fave

Caroline Stanbury of The Ladies of London, she received a text from an old friend.

Scoop. Now. Need exclusive. Where r u?

Piper's thumbs rapidly fired back: *Starbucks drive-thru.*

Be there in 5. Thx.

As much as Piper wanted to see Rusty, she couldn't help but give in to her friend's request. After handing the guy at the window exact change for a piping hot cup of joe, she pulled her car into the nearest parking spot. Rusty would just have to wait for his boring black coffee until later. Inside the coffee shop, she found an empty table in the corner by the restroom. With her trademark skinny vanilla latte firmly in hand, she took a seat. Minutes later, the sound of the adjacent glass door opening jarred her from a reverie of thoughts. A lanky guy in his mid-twenties, clad in a preppy sweater, straight-legged jeans, and alligator loafers slipped into the opposite-facing chair. A broad smile covered his face.

"Well, look who the cat dragged in! Mr. Preppy golf pro wannabe turned newspaper reporter! What's new on the beat?" she teased.

"You tell me, library board president killer!" he jested.

"Hush right now, Jay Baker! I did not kill Brandt. I just found his pitiful dead body, that's all."

The commotion from the pair caused the folks in the coffee shop to pause mid-sip for a quick looksee in their direction. Both Piper and Jay faked a pleasant smile and then continued with their private discussion.

"I need an exclusive, Piper. I've been on the job for about a month now and I haven't brought in any newsworthy tips. I'm hearing the gossipers around the office saying I only got this job because my dad owns the paper."

"But, isn't that true?" Piper took a sip of her java.

Jay put his hands on his hips. "Well, to a certain extent. But that's not the point. I'm a good writer. I earned a B+ in Mr. Burkey's English class."

"Only a B+?" Piper chided him.

Piper first had the pleasure of meeting Jay two years ago at the Woodlawn Golf & Country Club. As the golf pro in training, he had a rather scandalous reputation for keeping bored housewives occupied while their husbands were busy entertaining clients of their own. His schedule remained steadily booked until the downturn in the economy resulted in his position being eliminated. With the lack of prior job experience, he had no other choice but to join the family business.

"He's a really hard grader. C'mon, Piper, your misfortune has the potential to become my big break. By the way, do you mind if I go order a cup of coffee?" Jay started to get up from his chair only to be pushed right back down by his cohort in crime. "I'm taking that as a no." He sulked.

Piper checked the time on her cell phone. "Okay, fine. I'll tell you what I know, but you can't use my name in the story."

"Whose name should I use then?" His deadpan expression relayed his ignorance. Poised with a shiny new pen in his hand, Jay sat perched in place ready for action.

Piper patted his fair skinned hand. "Write down these words. *From a reliable source…*"

During the next ten minutes, Piper flushed out a fact-driven story, peppered with tidbits of unessential sidebars to enhance the overall picture of what had taken place. Jay took copious notes, stopping maybe once or twice to question what Piper had shared. When she thought he'd gathered a satisfactory amount of fodder, she pulled the plug on their clandestine rendezvous. Piper reiterated the importance of her involvement remaining anonymous so that Capt. Morgan would not hunt her down for opening her big mouth to the press. In return, Jay didn't mention Piper's scraggly hair or lack of make-up.

With Rusty's coffee forgotten, the friends sauntered out of the building arm in arm, pleased with their exchange of information. Little did they know that the murderer had been seated just a few tables away.

Chapter 5
Treasurer's Report

The rumor mill churned with excitement the next morning with a smattering of theories circulating between the stacks. The patrons sparked up conversations with the librarians under the pretense of checking out books in the hope of garnering some inside scoop. Larry emailed his staff a lengthy memo stating under no circumstances should his employees be engaging in dubious conversations centering on speculation and hearsay. He also summoned the members of the board of trustees to assemble in the meeting room at eleven o'clock sharp. The media set up camp outside the front entrance thanks to the late night news blast Jay posted on the Patchwork website, alerting the public to the crisis at hand. Between the media hounds breathing down his neck and the overall stress of the present situation, Larry's illness seemed to take on a life of its own. Between coughing spasms and the constant demand for his attention, the building pressure boxed him into a tight corner with no signs of escaping.

Across town, Piper sat on her front stoop quenching her insatiable thirst with a cold bottle of water. Her morning walk drained all the energy from her body. After having strategized most of the night over plausible suspects with Rusty, Piper needed a break from the chaos to refocus and simply catch her breath. Tattooed in her memory lingered the image of Brandt's trapped corpse. No matter how hard she tried, she couldn't erase it. Her phone lit up with a constant stream of texts, tweets, and calls from just about everyone she knew wanting the inside scoop on all things murder-related. To get away from it all, Piper turned it off and left it inside on the kitchen counter until later. Even her kitty, Ralph Lauren, could sense her uneasiness as he sidled up alongside his owner in search of a backrub. Sure enough, the last person Piper wanted to see that morning happened to take a stroll down her street. Piper ducked her sweaty head while crossing her fingers she hadn't been spotted. No such luck. The vixen evidently had eyes in the back of her head.

"Hey, Piper! Is that you?" The modelesque figure paused, pivoted, and then approached Piper's front stoop in long, graceful strides. "Looks like you've already been exercising. Too bad. We could've worked out together."

Piper slowly tilted her chin up and then peered over the top of the water bottle. "Hey, Desiree." Those two simple words zapped any remaining energy she had left. Desiree waited for Piper to say something else, but no words escaped her lips. Just a sigh of exhaustion and an empty stare.

Desiree scrunched up her face. "Okay, then. So, will I see you later at the board meeting? Larry has a full agenda in store."

Piper tilted her head. "I suppose so. Are you going?"

Desiree mistook Piper's response as an open invitation to join her on the stoop. Piper's body language spoke volumes as she inched closer to the edge and made a grimacing face.

"Well, um, yes. We need to discuss the Booklovers' Ball. I sent the Evites out this morning, per Larry's request. The online registration is open and about one hundred or so tickets have already been spoken for.

Also, I completed a budget analysis for the event that the board needs to review. "

"Yes, I'm well aware of what you've been up to." Piper's initial reason for stopping by Larry's office pertained to that such report.

"Plus, due to Brandt's unfortunate demise, Judge Halbreath will now need to assume the duties of chairperson and Chuck Loudon will become the vice-chair. That leaves the treasurer's position wide open. Any idea who might be interested in serving?"

Piper's limp body instantly became ramrod straight. It was as if someone had pulled a string from the top of her head like a marionette. She perked right up.

"Me!" She raised her hand in the air like a school girl. "I'll do it! I'd be perfect for the job." She couldn't contain her excitement. Full access to the financial wherewithals of the library meant she could dig deep and find out what happened to the missing funds without anyone suspecting what she was doing. Piper stood up and pointed to her house. "I really need to get inside and shower. I don't want to be late for the meeting."

Desiree said, "But, it's only nine thirty, and the meeting isn't until eleven."

Piper twitched her lips. "Okay, well that gives me almost enough time to get ready. It was good talking with you. See you later." She gave Desiree a gentle push to send her on her way. Before the woman could respond, Piper crossed the threshold of her home and closed the door behind her.

In less than thirty seconds flat, Piper dialed up Rusty in order to fill him in on her plan. The two exchanged strategies on how to convince the others that Piper would make the best candidate from among the bunch. Her main competition would come from Carolyn whether she wanted the position or not. Piper needed to smooth things over with her prior to the meeting so that the queen bee of the country club wouldn't inadvertently botch her plan. She had plenty of experience dealing with Carolyn from which to draw upon. Piper typed an ambiguous text asking Carolyn to meet fifteen minutes before the meeting in the library's parking lot. Within mere seconds, Carolyn responded with three simple words, *I guess so*. Piper's veiled request piqued Carolyn's curiosity just enough that she was willing to take the bait. Ready for action, Piper scurried up the staircase to shower and primp before the big event.

Back at the library, a constant stream of visitors kept the librarians busier than ever since the doors had opened at nine o'clock. Townsfolk who never stepped foot in the building now had a keen interest in all things library related. The staff kept a constant watch on the back hallway allowing no press or patrons access to the restricted area. Mrs. B. and Larry were temporarily relocated to the study room in a makeshift office until Capt. Morgan gave the thumbs up for them to return to their designated space. The hazmat cleaning company was able to complete their job despite the brazen interruption by Nancy, the president of the Friends group. Without permission, she barged into Larry's office demanding the crew halt midstream while she riffled through Larry's desk in search of something important. With papers in hand, she exited the area and then locked herself in the staff break room much to the chagrin of the others. By the time her little episode was brought to Larry's attention, she'd been long gone from the library.

Around ten thirty, the board members began trickling into the building. Rev. Black led the procession, attired in his customary black suit with a white collar. He flashed his signature dimples to the crowd as they gathered around to greet the charming bachelor. From young vixens to old maids, he mesmerized the room with his dry wit and charming good looks. Even when it poured, the man reigned from his imaginary throne no matter what the circumstances.

Next to arrive was Chuck Loudon, the curmudgeon board member and nemesis to the beloved reverend. His grim expression warded off any contact from the large crowd. The burly hardware store owner made his way over to the audiobooks where he browsed over the selection of new releases. His close proximity to Rev. Black didn't matter. Neither man would acknowledge the other solely on principle. The pair often butted heads amid heated debates behind closed boardroom doors.

The sliding glass doors opened, welcoming January Mitchell among the teeming masses. She sashayed between the aisles with her long, gauzy skirt leading the way. Unlike Chuck, she took the opportunity to chat with acquaintances and library workers expressing a genuine interest in their well-being. Adorned in a signature green scarf pinned with an antique brooch, her easy style and timeless fashion complimented her laid back persona.

In comparison, Judge Halbreath made a grand mid-morning entrance attired in a conservative black suit, crisp white shirt, sturdy black shoes, and a worn briefcase bursting with files. A nod and wave to folks in various corners of the room did little to slow her down as she navigated her approach towards the boardroom. A woman on a mission best described this career-driven doyenne who found it difficult to allocate time for petty socializing when duty called.

Parked in the rear of the building, Piper waited for Carolyn to arrive. In true prima donna fashion, Carolyn appeared to be running late. With every passing minute,

Piper checked her watch and then her phone for texts. First she started nibbling on her fingernails. Next, she folded and then unfolded her hands. Her bad habits did little to calm her nerves. To pass the time, she rehearsed the lines to the best of her recollection that she had written before taking off for the library. She kicked herself for leaving that scrap of paper behind. When Carolyn's car finally came in view, Piper came unglued. She unrolled the passenger's side window and frantically waved for her to come over. Carolyn scurried over to the vehicle in her four-inch heels, laden down by her cavernous designer purse. As soon as she parked herself in the seat, Piper poured on the charm in an effort to form an alliance with the one woman who had the ability to irk her most.

Carolyn knitted her brows as she listened to Piper go on and on about all the reasons why she would make an excellent candidate for the treasurer's position. Finally, she could take no more.

"Piper, let's be real here. I've known you for about three years now, right?"

Piper nodded her head in agreement.

Carolyn continued, "Not once can I remember you having a knack for numbers. Case in point, don't you recall your need for an electronic scorekeeper when we played together in the ladies' nine hole group? C'mon, what are you really up to?" She viewed Piper through slanted eyes.

The blonde mulled it over for less than a few seconds and then blurted out, "I think I know who killed Brandt. I need access to the library's financial records to prove it."

Carolyn threw her arms up in the air. "Oh, here we go again. Why can't you ever leave well enough alone? Capt. Morgan is more than capable of doing his job. Why not spend your time worrying about the latest styles off the runway rather than pretending to solve a murder case?" Carolyn reached for the door handle.

Piper leaned over and braced her arm across the woman's surgically-enhanced bosom, preventing her from exiting the car. "If you help me get elected, I'll let you pick out the décor for the ball. No questions asked."

Carolyn relaxed. "It would be nice not to quibble over details. How about my name is listed as chair and you as part of the committee, but you still have to help in whatever capacity I choose?"

"Yes!" Piper held out her right hand. The two sealed the deal with a firm handshake.

And with that, they gathered their belongings and headed into the building walking side by side. As they made their way into the boardroom, Larry began instructing the group to take their assigned seats in preparation for the meeting. Mrs. B. was finishing up her duty of placing the name placards identifying each board member at their designated spot. As soon as she had moved away from the U shaped table, the group obliged Larry's request. Brandt's absence was duly noted by all in attendance for his name sat staring back at them from the head of the table. At first, no one dared to speak. All eyes rested on Larry to dictate the proper protocol for such a somber gathering. Even Chuck did his best to smother a yawn out of respect for the dearly departed. The minutes ticked by without anyone breaking the silence. Finally, Judge Halbreath gave a faint nod to Mrs. B. It was almost a blessing, if you will. A bit of relief mingled with sadness hung heavily in the air. Mrs. B quietly stated there was a quorum, signaling for the meeting to begin.

Judge Halbreath struck the gavel. "Good morning. This emergency meeting is now called to order. Are there any changes to the agenda?"

Mrs. B. spoke up. "There are not."

"Well, then," Judge Halbreath continued, "we must address the matter at hand. The board publicly extends its condolences to the Dixon family. There will be a private memorial service followed by internment at the Woodlawn Memorial Gardens within the next couple of days. In lieu of flowers, the family has requested donations in remembrance of Brandt to be made to the Woodlawn Art Society. The board will honor his memory with a monetary contribution to his charity as well as erect a small placard here in the public meeting room commemorating his many contributions to the library system."

Reverend Black bowed his head in homage to the former president of the board. The rest of his peers followed suit as they paused for a brief moment of silence.

Judge Halbreath cleared her throat signaling the conclusion of the touching tribute. "Per our by-laws, we must fill the vacant position. As vice-chairperson, I will now assume the duties of chair. That means Chuck Loudon will then become the vice-chair leaving the treasurer's position open. Do I have any nominations for this position?"

Reverend Black spoke up. "I nominate January Mitchell."

The judge said, "January, would you like your name added to the ballot?"

January nodded in agreement.

"Any others?" Judge Halbreath asked.

Piper gave the evil eye to Carolyn. The woman smirked and then said, "I nominate Piper O'Donnell."

Judge Halbreath raised her eyebrows in surprise. "Piper? Hmm." She turned her head in Piper's direction. "Are you up for such a task?"

Piper puffed up her chest and firmly stated, "I am."

The group snickered among themselves.

Judge Halbreath ignored their disapproving grumbles. "Any other nominations?" No one said a word.

"Okay then, Mrs. B., would you mind passing out slips of paper to the members? I think it's best if we vote anonymously."

Mrs. B. made some makeshift ballots out of some leftover raffle tickets she had stuffed in her binder. She carefully counted out six. She then went around the table and handed one to each person. As soon as they were finished casting their votes, she retraced her steps and gathered the votes in the palm of her hand.

"Since we only have six board members at this juncture, if there is a tie, Larry will be called upon to cast the deciding vote. This election affects him the most since the director and executive committee work hand in hand governing the library. Mrs. B., have you tallied up the votes?"

Mrs. B. affirmed so by nodding her head.

Judge Halbreath asked, "Do we have a clear winner?"

"We do," she replied in an official sounding voice.

All eyes rested on the spry woman holding the fate of the election in her hands.

The prominent judge drew in a deep breath and then proceeded to say, "Mrs. B., please announce the results."

Rather than simply stating the winner, Mrs. B. chose to drag it out a tad longer much to the chagrin of the others. She stood up, straightened her skirt, and then gently placed her reading glasses on the bridge of her nose. For full effect, she cleared her throat and then unveiled the winner. "January Mitchell...,"

A big smile lit up January's face. She stole a glance in Piper's direction.

Mrs. B. continued, "earned two votes. Piper O'Donnell had four. Congratulations, Piper. You have been elected the new treasurer of the board."

"You've got to be kidding me! I demand a recount!" January flew out of her seat. The disputatious board member had much experience engaging in heated debates over the years mostly ending favorably and on her own terms. Being on the losing side of the battle was uncharted territory for this veteran colleague.

Rather than forking over the ballots, Mrs. B. snatched them right off the table. Her ominous stare dared January to challenge her authority. All the while this exchange was taking place, Piper remained quietly in her seat. Like a spectator at a sporting event, she took everything in without getting personally involved in the present situation. Finally, Denise Halbreath stepped up and took control of the meeting.

"Mrs. B., please bring me the ballots. I would like to count them myself if you don't mind."

In a meek little old lady's voice she replied, "Of course, Judge Halbreath." Mrs. B. strode over to the woman's side and placed two piles neatly in front of her.

Piper cracked a smile. The woman's obedience to the judge was a calculating attempt to make January look like a villain. Piper held Mrs. B.'s gaze in a silent affirmation of sheer admiration. The executive assistant turned on her heels and then resumed her seat at the table.

Slowly, the new president of the board of trustees read aloud the name printed on each ballot for all to hear. January cringed every time Piper's name was mentioned. The process didn't take long seeing as there were only six of them eligible to vote. As expected, Judge Halbreath declared Piper as the official winner.

January gave up the fight and shrugged her shoulders in defeat.

In an effort to move on, Piper accepted her new office with a gracious thank you to her fellow board members.

Taking advantage of having everyone together, Judge Halbreath publicly confirmed with Desiree that the evites had been sent and that on-line registration had begun, as requested by Brandt.

Carolyn reported to the group that she was in the throes of coordinating the decorations for the event. She also pointed out that in light of Piper's new position, she recommended that the board delegate her to serve on the committee rather than co-chairing as originally planned. Imagine the group's surprise when Piper wholeheartedly agreed.

The meeting concluded with Chuck's rumbling that he had an afternoon golf game to get to and could care less about froufrou decorations and such. Judge Halbreath asked to meet privately with Larry and the executive committee afterwards in order to get a handle on the upcoming committee reports. January and Reverend Black exited the room without expressing one word of goodbye.

As Piper got up from her chair, she couldn't help but notice an unusual pair whispering in private over in the far corner of the room.

"Piper, are you coming?" Judge Halbreath stood in the doorway motioning for her to join the others. "The meeting won't take very long," the woman assured her.

Piper hesitated for a brief moment. The sight of Carolyn and Desiree huddled together caused her stomach to churn. *Maybe I could just go over and ...*

"Piper?" Judge Halbreath interrupted her thoughts.

With no other choice Piper replied, "Yes, Judge Halbreath. Here I come."

Chapter 6
Committee Reports

Much to Piper's surprise, the executive meeting took place in Larry's office. The hazmat team had given Mrs. B. the go ahead to return to business as usual. Crossing the threshold felt like an out of body experience. Larry busied himself with clearing off cluttered spaces, making room for the four of them to congregate. Piper stood still, taking in the magnitude of being back in the room where the murder took place. Her gut reaction told her to turn away from the spot where she found Brandt lying face down on the floor. Never one to listen to her own inner voice, she peeked anyway. Piper breathed a sigh of relief when she realized there was no trace of blood on the carpet. Four chairs were assembled around Larry's desk. Piper chose to sit between Chuck and the judge.

"How long is this going to take, Denise?" Chuck fidgeted in his chair.

"We know. You have a tee time," Larry said matter-of-factly. "When do you ever work?"

Chuck dismissed Larry's sarcastic comment with a flip of his wrist.

Denise ignored both of them and got right down to business. "Seeing as the board is in flux, I think it's best if we conduct our own internal audit of the committees. Plus we need to establish the chairs, as well."

Larry spoke right up. "And, why is that necessary? I have been overseeing every committee on a regular basis. Just because Brandt is no longer with us doesn't mean we have to start picking things apart."

Piper noticed the beads of perspiration pooling on Larry's forehead. Now was the time to strike. "I do have some questions for you, Larry, if you don't mind."

Chuck butted right in. "Piper, dear. Larry will bring you up to speed on the financial aspects of the library sometime in the next couple of weeks. Desiree just completed a budget analysis for the ball. Until then, if you have any questions or concerns, please feel free to call upon me."

"Thank you, Chuck, for making yourself available to Piper. That's very kind of you," Denise commented.

"So, are we good to go?" Chuck's tee time took precedence over any library meeting.

"Not so fast," Denise said. "We need to appoint chairpersons for each of the standing committees. We intended to do that last week but Brandt got sidetracked by all of the hoopla concerning the naming of the library ball."

"Yes, we really need to get that squared away," insisted Larry. His composure appeared less tense.

Chuck grabbed a pad and pencil off of Larry's desk and began writing. "Fine. Let's make it snappy. Budget and Finance should be led by Piper. No brain there."

"Excuse me?" Piper squealed.

"I meant no brainer," Chuck corrected his facetious remark. "Of course, you should be in charge of that one." He and Larry swapped mischievous looks.

Denise interjected, "Let's move on. Executive committee will be steered by me. Capital Improvements...how about Reverend Black?"

"That should be a good fit," Piper added.

"Yes, his church is in the middle of a huge capital campaign. The man knows whose pockets are deep in this town. That could prove to be useful," Chuck pointed out.

"Now, how about human resources? That's a tricky one. We need someone who is rather diplomatic," Denise suggested.

Piper said, "That rules out Carolyn. She's been proven to be fickle at times. I nominate January. She seems to be tactful when necessary."

The group kept quiet.

"Okay, does anyone have a better suggestion?" Piper asked.

Denise interjected her opinion. "I believe Chuck is best suited for the job."

The others agreed.

"The last committee head we need to fill is the liaison to the Foundation which includes serving as the board's representative to the Friends group."

Not missing a beat Piper shouted, "Carolyn! Carolyn will do it."

Larry, Chuck, and Denise were taken aback by Piper's flagrant outburst.

"Fine," Denise simply replied. "If that's what you would like, I think we all are in agreement." The two men nodded their heads.

"So, are we finished here?" Chuck couldn't help but be a little pushy. The greens were on the foremost on his mind.

Larry spoke up, "Piper, I'll give you a call next week to set up a brief financial orientation. It shouldn't take more than thirty minutes."

"Better yet, why don't we coordinate our calendars now to save time? With the ball coming up, I want to be in the know." Piper grinned.

Chuck gathered up his belongings and headed towards the door. He wasn't waiting for permission from Denise to leave. Their conversation had nothing to do with him, or so he thought.

"Chuck," said Larry. "You might want to stick around for a few minutes. I think it would beneficial for you to meet with Piper and me since you know what's going on with the library's finances."

"Send me a text with times and dates. I'll get back to you," he bellowed over his shoulder. And with that, he was gone.

Piper and Larry agreed to meet tomorrow evening if Chuck's calendar permitted.

As they were headed out the door, Denise asked to speak with Larry privately. Piper happily obliged and said her goodbyes.

Once in the car, she could feel her tummy rumbling. With Rusty being occupied at the liquor store with the day's deliveries, Piper decided to make an impromptu drive-by to Dr. King's office where her sister Penelope worked part-time. If she timed it right, her sister should be on her way out the door. The two could catch up over lunch.

Sure enough, Piper spotted Penelope getting into her Lexus as soon as she turned the corner. She pulled up right alongside her and said, "Hey, sis! Want to join me for lunch?"

Penelope smiled, "Absolutely! How about we go to the diner?"

Piper nodded. "Good choice. Meet you there."

When they arrived, the place was hopping with hungry townsfolk craving good old-fashioned comfort food. The sisters cozied up in a small booth in the corner, a good distance from the noisy lunch crowd. Their favorite waitress Suzy greeted them with two sweet teas and a couple of worn menus. Being regular customers had its perks.

"Need a few minutes?" the cheerful blonde asked.

"I don't know why we even bother pretending to read this. I'll have the usual," Piper handed back the menu.

"Turkey club for you, too, Penelope?" Suzy smacked her pink bubblegum.

"Please, and two side salads," she requested.

Suzy collected her menu. "You got it, sugar."

Piper glanced at her phone. "No missed messages or texts. I'm surprised. What with everything that's going on, I thought for sure Jay would be looking for me."

Penelope unfolded the paper napkin that held the silverware. She placed the fork, knife, and spoon on the table and then covered her lap with the napkin. "I'm assuming you were his anonymous tip?"

"What makes you think that, sis?" Piper tried to act coy.

"Really? You two are thick as thieves. Although, he did a nice job trying to pretend he has an "in" at the police station." She made quotation marks with her fingers to emphasize it. "I know this murder thing is your number one priority right now, but do you think we could talk about something else instead? I have some big news." Penelope cocked her head to one side pleading for her sister to give in to her request. She rested her hands on Piper's forearm that was leaning on the table.

Piper nudged her sister. "Sure. Why not? My brain is on overload from the library meeting I just left anyway. What's up?"

Penelope paused for a second as Suzy served the sisters their petite green salads.

"Thank you," the sisters said in unison.

"My pleasure!" Suzy snatched the straw wrappers off the table, crumbled them up, and stashed the little pieces of paper in the front pocket of her apron. "Anything else I can get you?" She smiled.

"No, we're good," Piper answered.

Suzy nodded her head and continued on to the next table.

"I quit my job!" Penelope announced. She could barely contain herself.

Piper stopped midway to her mouth with a forkful of salad. "What?"

"Got your attention with that one, huh?" Penelope poked her older sister.

"It's about time, actually. I'm proud of you, sis. What made you do it? Did you catch Dr. King with some leggy bimbo?" Piper made no bones about her dislike for the playboy doctor.

"C'mon, Piper. He's not that bad." Penelope took a bite of her salad. She followed it with a swig of sweet tea. "I'm starting a new job tomorrow."

"Really?" Piper wiped her mouth with the napkin. "Where?"

"It's a gallery on Main Street. I think I'll be selling paintings and organizing art shows. Finally, I'll be able to put my college education to good use. I told mom and dad my art major would come in handy one day."

Piper choked on her sweet tea.

"Are you okay?" Penelope patted Piper on her back.

"I'm fine. I'm fine. Did you say an art gallery on Main Street?" Piper couldn't believe her ears.

Penelope had a puzzling look on her face. "Yes, why? Is there something wrong with that?"

Her defensive tone caught Piper off guard. "No, not at all. Who hired you?" Piper just had to know.

Suzy butted in before Penelope had a chance to respond. "Lunch is served. Two turkey club sandwiches with a side of honey mustard on each plate. May I bring you anything else?"

"No, thank you." Piper answered for both of them.

As soon as Suzy was out of earshot, Piper continued, "So, who hired you?"

Penelope rolled her eyes. "I don't see what difference it makes, but if you have to know, some guy named Brandt."

Piper gasped.

"What's wrong?" Penelope latched on to her arm.

Piper grabbed Penelope's elbows and pulled her closer. "That's whose body I found!"

"Holy…"

Piper covered Penelope's mouth with her hand. "And, I think someone killed him because he knew exactly who's responsible for the misappropriated funds. Now that you're working there, you can be my informant."

Penelope claps her hands. "Awesome! I've always wanted to play a detective in a movie. Now here's my chance." She took a generous bite of her sandwich.

"Here's the thing," Piper continued. "Not sure if you knew this or not, but Brandt was gay."

Penelope rolled her eyes. "That man was better dressed than half the women we know."

"I know, right? So, listen. His partner, I'm sure, is absolutely devastated by the news. Have you met him?" Piper dipped her sandwich in some honey mustard sauce and then took a bite. "Mmm. So delish."

"Yes, I did meet him. He was there when Brandt interviewed me for the position. His name is Shep Stewart. Tall, dark-haired man with a fabulous complexion. Needs to lay off the fake tanning lotion, but besides that he seems like a nice guy." Penelope waved Suzy over for a refill of sweet tea.

Out of the corner of her eye Piper spotted a shrouded figure heading in their direction. The person wore a baggy trench coat and on top of his head perched a crumpled fedora. Piper nudged her sister to take a gander just as the individual slid alongside her in the u-shaped booth.

"Jay Baker, what kind of outfit is this?" Piper flicked his hat right off of his head, uncovering a mishmash of hair.

'Hey, hey, hey! Watch it! You're blowing my cover." Jay grabbed his black fedora and with both hands pulled it down over his unruly mane.

Piper chuckled. "Want part of my sandwich?" She handed him a peace offering.

Jay snatched it up and said, "It's best for me to remain incognito. I need an anonymous tip on the murder story. My dad's breathing down my neck for some newsworthy bit of information."

Suzy strolled up alongside the table and said, "Hey, Jay. Would you like a diet soda?"

Jay scowled. "How did you know it was me?"

Suzy leaned in close enough for him to get a bird's eye view of her cleavage, "Lucky guess." She winked. "Be back with your drink in a couple of minutes."

The sisters giggled over Suzy's schoolgirl crush.

Jay ignored their childish behavior and removed his wrinkled trench coat. Stuffing it between Piper and himself, he continued. "So Piper, what's new with the case? Give me something good." He munched down on his portion of the turkey club.

"Funny you should ask." She handed him a napkin and pointed to the corner of her mouth to let him know he had dribbled. "Penelope has a new job," she said.

Jay wiped the mayo off of his face. "Congratulations! But, what does that have do with Brandt's murder?" He finished it off with one last bite.

Piper whispered, "She's working at the gallery with his *partner* Shep."

"Bingo!" Jay could barely contain his excitement. He whipped out a tiny scratchpad and a nubby pencil.

Jotting down some notes he asked, "When do you start, Penelope?"

She finished swallowing a swig of sweet tea and then replied, "Tomorrow. I have an orientation with Shep before the gallery opens. With Brandt being…um…not there anymore, I wonder what my position will exactly entail. I betcha I'll have more responsibility. Maybe even be promoted to like assistant store manager! Do you think I should like pretend I don't even know he was killed? Kinda like play dumb?"

Jay thought for a few seconds before offering up his opinion. "I don't think that would be much of a stretch for you."

Piper jabbed his arm. "Did you really just say that to my sister?"

"I didn't mean to be facetious. Her being employed at the gallery is huge. Yes, we need her to play dumb. C'mon. With her flowing blonde hair and perfect figure, she could pass for a bimbo,"

Penelope gave him the evil eye.

"Which you certainly are not," he clarified. "Think of it as an acting job."

Piper added her two cents. "You've always said you wanted to be a movie star."

"True," Penelope conceded.

Jay stole a crouton from Piper's salad. "Seriously, girls. Just hear me out. The less Shep thinks she knows, the more he'll be willing to divulge. You need to become his confidante. Shopping buddy. Whatever it takes to earn his trust. And it goes without saying… your number one priority will be to report back to me. My job is riding on it, sweetheart."

"One step at a time," Piper said.

For the next ten minutes, the partners in crime strategized in hushed snippets of conversation. Piper vetoed a couple of Jay's harebrained suggestions along with a few of Penelope's crazy cloak and dagger schemes. All the while Suzy circled the table like a hawk trying her best to hurry them along. Hovering close by, impatient townsfolk waited for tables to free up. Piper signaled for the check when she realized the dream team was getting nowhere. Jay excused himself for a quick trip to the men's room while Piper settled the bill. Upon his return, Piper pinky promised Jay to call him should she hear of any new developments.

"I need to make a quick trip to the ladies' room before I leave. You two go ahead," Piper insisted. She stuffed the receipt into her purse.

"Thanks for lunch." Penelope kissed her sister goodbye on the cheek.

As for Jay, he threw on his hat and coat and scooted towards the back door. He didn't bother saying goodbye to the sisters, for clearly he'd resumed his sly newspaper reporter persona. Yet unbeknownst to him, the other diners in the restaurant couldn't help but stare. As he made his imaginary getaway, a long piece of toilet paper remained firmly stuck to the bottom of one of his worn brown shoes.

On her way to the restroom, Piper spotted Reverend Black in a corner booth dining with a male friend. At first, she thought about going over and saying hello, but then thought better of it for it appeared as if they were involved in a deep discussion of sorts. On second glance, she realized it was more like a heated exchange. With her curiosity piqued, Piper veered to the left. "Reverend Black! Is that you?"

The two men halted their conversation.

She cozied right up alongside their table. Piper politely smiled to his tablemate only to have it returned with a sour puss. Instead, she redirected her attention back to the man in black.

"Well, hello, Piper. So good to see you. Are you dining here today?" Rev. Black turned on his preacher charm.

Piper played along, "Just finished." She turned to Mr. Cranky Pants. "I don't think we've had the pleasure of meeting. My name is Piper O'Donnell. And you are..." She extended her well-manicured hand.

"Shep. Shep Stewart," the roguish gent muttered as he returned the handshake.

Piper beamed. "Really? You don't say..."

Chapter 7
Special Presentations

By the time Piper left the diner, she was bursting at the seams. Having the chance to talk with Shep one on one proved to be invaluable. Reverend Black expressed his disdain for her blatant intrusion on their private lunch, but on cue Piper chose to ignore his frequent attempts to send her away. Halfway through their conversation, she fully acknowledged being the one who found Brandt's lifeless body. Amid tears, Shep reminisced about the good times he shared with his partner in life and business. Not once did Piper mention that she was related to Penelope. A bold move that could prove to be dangerous in the near future but one she had to take. Rev. Black spent the majority of the time on his Blackberry catching up on emails which seemed to suit Piper and Shep just fine. The two gabbed like bosom buddies. The impromptu meeting came to a close when Suzy brought over the check. Shep gave Piper a bear hug and thanked her a couple times for stopping by. Rev. Black offered a weak smile as his goodbye salutation which was more than generous considering she had crashed their luncheon.

First stop on her victory tour was the liquor store. The parking lot was filled to capacity with luxury mobiles, beat up trucks, and eco-friendly compact cars. Piper pulled around back and parked in a vacant employee spot. She maneuvered the rearview mirror so that she could freshen up her makeup and apply some chubby stick lip color. She tousled her hair just enough to make it look sexy, but refined. Pleased with her speedy makeover, she exited the vehicle.

Inside, she was greeted by some familiar faces. Rusty's store had many loyal patrons despite the recent opening of a giant wholesale store located right outside of town. He was no dummy when it came to business sense. He stocked plenty of liquor for his repeat customers so that they never left his store empty-handed. He also cornered the market with the local restaurants serving as their main supplier. Specializing in fine wines and trendy alcohol, these days Rusty was at the top of his game.

It didn't take long for Rusty to spot his fiancée from across the store. Her golden blonde hair stood out like a ray of sunshine. The two made eye contact for a fleeting moment, and then Rusty resumed his duties of ringing up orders at the front check-out counter. Standing beside Rusty were two college-aged guys who worked part-time for him throughout the year. Both young men were attending school at Woodlawn Community College.

An elderly woman with a cardboard box jammed with expensive bottles of wine was giving Rusty a hard time over something to do with a coupon. Piper heard Rusty say something about it being the wrong brand. All she could decipher from the lady's high-pitched voice was something along the lines of "the wholesale store takes expired coupons." Within a couple of minutes, Rusty accepted the coupon and sent the woman on her merry way. Piper chuckled to herself because here was another example why the folks in Woodlawn kept coming back. Rusty's customers were always right.

Piper edged closer to the counter hoping to get a few minutes to talk with Rusty. No luck. A barrage of customers pushed her aside to get in line. Piper took it in stride and moseyed over to the wine section to browse the newest products. Her eyes lit up when she spotted LVP Sangria bottled by one of her favorite Real Housewives, Lisa Vanderpump. He even ordered both kinds—red and pink. She fondled the bottle of pink sangria, imagining the rich bouquet of flavors she would be savoring later on that evening. On the opposite side of the aisle, numerous Skinnygirl products lined the shelves. Piper felt a sense of pride that Rusty thought highly enough of her business expertise to stock her recommendations. As she'd told him many times, a happy wife is a happy life.

With the pink LVP Sangria in one hand and a bottle of Skinnygirl White Sangria in the other, Piper was ready to check out. Much to her disappointment, the line meandered towards the rear of the store. She rolled her eyes. Piper moved to the vodka aisle and texted Rusty.

Meet me in the back.

She waited a few minutes. No response. So, she tried again.

Meet me now. I have big news.

Still not a peep from her fiancé.

Piper tapped her high heel on the floor as she waited for Rusty to respond. A disheveled-looking woman standing in line did not appreciate the noise and shot her an ugly stare. Piper just turned around and kept tapping. Just then, her eye zeroed in on the solution to her woes. Twitching her lips, she contemplated whether her lack of patience merited what she was tempted to do. First, she took a quick headcount of the store. There were twenty-three customers in all monopolizing Rusty's time, keeping him from her. As she wondered if it was worth upsetting Rusty, her thoughts were interrupted by the shrill sound of the annoying woman's voice, complaining to her husband about the slow service and high prices of the store.

Seriously? she thought. That pushed Piper over the edge. She marched right back to the corner of the store and yanked the fire alarm. Immediately, the horns started blaring and the strobe lights flickered. Piper grabbed a folding chair from the office and planted herself in it. The two bottles of sangria she placed on the floor next to her feet. Panicked customers stashed their lots wherever they could find room. One shady character tried to sneak out the door with his booze, only to be tripped by Piper's long leg. Luckily for her, his six pack of beer landed squarely on her lap. Piper whipped out her cellphone and dialed the fire chief's personal cell phone to let him know it was a false alarm. No need for the trucks to come zooming down the street. Piper and the chief had a history, to say the least, so he chose to take her at her word. He did insist, though, that Rusty himself leave him a message verifying that all was well. Piper assured him that Rusty would.

The store emptied out in lightning speed, save Piper and her man. When the frazzled store owner came careening round the corner and noticed Piper sitting primly in a chair, his face turned a vibrant red. If it were physically possible, steam would have risen from his head. He put his hands on his hips and said, "What are you doing?"

"Waiting for you! I have so much to tell you." She held up the bottle of LVP Sangria. "Thanks for ordering this, babe. I can't wait to taste it." Piper placed it back on the floor, stood up, and walked over towards him.

"Did you pull the fire alarm?" He was not giving in to her charms.

She tiptoed closer and said, "Yes."

He folded his arms across his chest. "Why would you do such a thing?"

She inched closer. "You didn't answer my texts."

He removed his cell phone from his jean pocket and looked at the screen. "Oops! I see you did text me. Sorry. I was busy."

She nuzzled right into his broad chest and gently wrapped her arms around his neck. "I know. I had to do something to grab your attention." The couple stood nose to nose.

"How about next time, you do this instead." He kissed her on her plump lips.

Piper blushed. "I guess that would have been a better option."

He laughed. "You think? So, what's so special about your news? Did you stumble upon another dead body?"

She playfully smacked him on the arm.

"C'mon. That's a pretty good guess, seeing as you do have a sixth sense for finding dead bodies." He grabbed her hand and led her down the hall to his office.

"What about my sangria?" She tugged in the opposite direction.

Rusty said, "Leave it. You can get it on your way out the door."

"I'm leaving so soon?" she pouted.

Rusty embraced her in his arms again. "Babe, I do have a business to run. I need to open back up sometime today before the rumor mill starts speculating something more serious is going on here."

"Oh, that reminds me." She took out her phone, tapped a couple of screens, and then handed it to him. "Here. You need to call Chief Derbyshire and let him know the building is still standing. I kinda promised him you would."

He took the phone in his hands and said, "You have the chief on speed dial?"

Piper said, "Doesn't everyone?" with an air of disbelief.

Their conversation was brief and mostly one sided. Rusty kept repeating 'yes, sir' and nodded his head up and down. When he finally hung up, Rusty didn't look happy.

"I hope you're happy. That little episode of yours just cost me a hefty donation to the volunteer fire station." He cocked his eyebrow.

"Look on the bright side," Piper added. "At least it's tax deductible."

The couple continued their conversation snuggled together on the plaid couch in Rusty's office. Piper left no detail unsaid and asked for his take on the situation more times than not. Rusty scolded his girlfriend for not telling Shep that she and Penelope were related. He stressed it was always best to be completely transparent when it came to garnering an ally. Piper shrugged it off as an insignificant piece of the puzzle and told him he was being paranoid. Rusty cautioned her to be careful. There was a killer on the loose who wouldn't take so kindly to her butting in on the situation.

Since Rusty wasn't telling Piper what she wanted to hear, she decided to split. On her way out, she swiped the bottles of sangria resting beside the folding chair. Sure enough, when she exited the front door, there were customers milling about in the parking lot waiting for the store to reopen. Piper buzzed right by the assembly and slipped into her black car.

All of a sudden, her phone vibrated signifying an incoming call. She didn't recognize the number, so she was tempted to send it over to voicemail. On the last ring, she changed her mind. "Hello, Piper? January Mitchell here. Do you have a few minutes?"

Piper wasn't certain what to say. Nothing ever associated with Jan took only a few minutes. "Hey, Jan. I'm just leaving the liquor store. What can I do for you?" She revved up the car's engine for full effect.

Jan paused and then said, "Having a bad day? You might want to consider taking up yoga. It'll calm your nerves and restore the Zen in your life."

Here we go again, she thought. *Another Jan Knows Best lecture. Her specialty.* Piper did not mince words. "No, Jan. My fiancé owns the liquor store. Remember? I stopped by to see him."

"Oh," she piped up. "I just left the post office. The head clerk told me about the evacuation. A bomb threat in Woodlawn, of all places. Do the police have any leads? Is your fiancé worried for his safety?"

"A bomb threat? My goodness, that couldn't be further from the truth," Piper insisted.

Jan wouldn't let up. "Then what did happen? Set the record straight."

Piper stumbled for a minute and then blurted, "A fire drill! It was a mandatory fire drill. Rusty takes seriously the safety of his customers. "

Jan didn't say a word. Piper took that as a good sign and continued on. "So, back to the reason for your call. What's on your mind?"

Jan did her patented disclaimer. "I didn't believe for a second that there was a bomb threat. It was all coming from the clerk, not me. I was an innocent bystander."

"Oh, for the love of God, what do you want, Jan? Spit it out." Piper could take no more.

Startled by her bluntness, Jan said, "Shep Stewart is having a special presentation at his gallery tonight for the library ball. We need to select the paintings that we will be auctioning off. Of course, we committed to splitting the proceeds with the gallery, so it's a win-win for everyone involved. Seeing as Brandt is no longer with us, I need the approval from someone else on the board. Rev. Black has a pastoral commitment, Judge Halbreath is busy, Chuck flat out said no, and Carolyn is cuckoo over the decorations. That leaves you. Would you be able to spare some time?"

"Sure." Piper waited.

"Is that a yes?" Jan asked.

"Yes," Piper confirmed.

"Splendid. Shep asked for us to be there at seven. It shouldn't take any longer than an hour. Then, we'll be on our way. He has some new girl starting tomorrow, so he wants to get this out of the way and the shop in order before she starts."

For the second time, Piper said nothing about being related to Penelope.

Jan droned on for nearly ten minutes concerning her artistic vision and how she wanted to incorporate up and coming artists in the exhibition. Piper contributed little to the conversation, nursing her ego after the small beating it took from being Jan's last choice. The two agreed to meet outside the gallery at ten minutes to seven. Jan was a stickler for being on time.

Piper decided to return home for a late afternoon snooze. Although the antibiotics were knocking out her sinus infection, a quick glance in the mirror confirmed the need for some beauty sleep. Her ruddy skin cried out for help. A combination of cool cucumber slices paired with a clarifying mask would do the trick. The thought of relaxing under the covers far away from the chaos soothed her tired soul.

Once inside her home, she found her precocious tomcat, Ralph Lauren, tucked between two cushions on her pristine, white couch. His designated throw blanket lay on the opposite end showing no signs of usage, typical of her entitled feline who ruled the roost. Rather than reprimand the pussy cat, Piper tickled his furry mane on her way up to the master bedroom. He retaliated with a low hiss. Indeed, Mr. Lauren hit the kitty lottery when Piper rescued him from the local animal shelter. The cat was spoiled rotten.

Upstairs, Piper lingered in the shower, washing away the stressors from the day. After toweling off, she assembled her beauty regimen on the marble countertop. The cool mud mask calmed her face. She quickly traipsed downstairs to retrieve some cucumber slices from the kitchen to complete her spa treatment. Rather than trudge back up to her boudoir, she decided to crash Ralph's party by collapsing on the sofa. Much to Piper's surprise, he snuggled right up with his owner. It didn't take long for the two kindred spirits to doze off.

If it weren't for the leaf blowers from next door, their slumber party might have lasted more than twenty minutes. The grumpy pair ambled off the couch, bothered by the incessant noise. Side by side, they peeked through the wooden slats. It appeared an army of lawn guys were invading her neighbor's property. Piper slammed the blinds shut and then plopped herself on the floor. Just then, her doorbell rang.

"Really?" Piper dragged her tired derrière off the floor. Her partner in crime, on the other hand, took off like a shot. Ralph was not a big fan of visitors. Piper tightened the belt on her pink fluffy bathrobe while grumbling on her way to the door. Through the peep hole, she spotted the source of the disruption. Piper clenched her teeth.

"Piper? I know you're in there. Open up!" the voice demanded.

Piper took hold of the heavy door and swung it open with all her might.

Her visitor squawked, "What the heck happened to you? Fall in a vat of mayonnaise?"

"Don't you know it's polite to call first before showing up unannounced at someone's house?" she reprimanded her visitor.

"Would you have answered the phone?" the guest replied.

Piper didn't skip a beat. "Heck, no."

"That's exactly why I didn't." Her company walked in the door.

Piper gave up. "So, what do I owe the pleasure of your company today, Capt. Morgan?"

He followed her to the kitchen and made himself right at home. "Want a cup of coffee?" he asked as he turned on her Keurig. "I think I'll try this Columbian Dark. Any good?"

"It's Rusty's favorite. Personally, I don't like the rich flavor," Piper volunteered.

Capt. Morgan removed a coffee mug from the rack resting next the machine. "I'm feeling lucky. I'll give it a try. Sure you don't want me to brew you some tea or hot cocoa?"

"No, thanks." Piper seated herself at the kitchen table. She cleared off some space to make room for her soon-to-be father-in-law. "So what's going on with the case?"

With a piping hot cup of joe in his hand, he replied, "Shouldn't I be asking the questions?"

"Technically, yes, but with us being practically related, I think that exempts us from following protocol," she insisted. Piper checked her phone for messages.

"Am I boring you?" he asked. Capt. Morgan sipped his coffee.

"Just seeing if I missed anything." She chucked her phone on the table.

Capt. Morgan peered at her. "Maybe you should go wash your face. It looks like whatever you smothered all over your skin formed a crust." He leaned in and flicked some of the gunk off of her chin with his fingernail.

Piper retaliated by swatting him with her hand. "Leave me alone. I'm detoxifying my skin."

He took a long gulp of coffee. "Let's get down to business, Piper."

She hoisted her feet up on an adjacent kitchen chair. "I'm listening."

Capt. Morgan confided in Piper that he hadn't made much progress tracking down Brandt's assailant. The rumor mill didn't help him any. The old biddies at the salon had plenty to say and not much of it was positive. To make matters worse, the police chief demanded Capt. Morgan choke up a list of suspects or else. As of that morning, Capt. Morgan had yet to compile an index of plausible names. Turning up on Piper's doorstep was the last thing he wanted to do, but he desperately needed her help.

"Well it's about time you realized that I could be helpful. Just ask Rusty!" She smiled from ear to ear.

Capt. Morgan fidgeted in his chair.

Piper looked at him wiggle about like a child. "What's the matter?"

He scratched his head. "Here's the thing. You can't let anyone know we're working on this together. And, you have to promise not to share what we discuss with your sister. She needs to be kept *completely* in the dark."

Piper snapped her head around. "What? Why? That doesn't make sense. We tell each other everything. We're sisters for heaven's sakes. That's absolutely ridiculous!"

"Maybe not everything..." his voice trailed off.

Piper's face flushed with anger. "What exactly are you insinuating? That's my sister you're talking about, mister!" She folded her arms across her chest waiting for a reply.

Capt. Morgan hesitated for a brief moment and then delivered the devastating news. "Penelope was spotted leaving the scene of the crime at the approximate time of Brandt's murder. As of now, she's my one and only suspect."

Chapter 8
Associate Director's Report

"Blood is thicker than water. Blood is thicker than water," Piper chanted aloud. She paced back and forth in her kitchen with a wild look in her eye. "Who does he think he is coming over to *my home* and dropping a bomb like that? And then, he just gets up and leaves like nothing at all happened. The nerve of him!" Piper often talked to herself behind closed doors. It helped her cope when she teetered on the edge of hysteria. Better to have a breakdown in the privacy of her home rather than in public for all the hungry gossipers to see. Piper grabbed her phone and began dialing her sister's number and then stopped. She stashed the phone in her bathrobe and dashed upstairs to her bedroom.

Again, she tried to dial her sister, but at the last second she couldn't pull the trigger. Piper chucked the phone in the middle of her dreamy king-sized bed and marched into the bathroom. She turned the water faucet on so that she could finally rinse off the facial mask. As she pressed the warm washcloth up against her face, it cleansed her tortured soul. Keeping a secret from her sister felt like the ultimate betrayal, especially being the eldest. Her role should be to protect her younger sister, not deceive.

Right then and there, Piper made the decision to go along with Capt. Morgan. Two could play this game of chicanery. If she could find evidence to prove to him that her sister was innocent without spilling the beans, then Capt. Morgan would be forced to eat crow. That in itself was motivation enough. Piper just hoped that when it was all said and done, Penelope would find it in her heart to forgive her. Keeping this secret bottled up would not be possible, so a phone call to Rusty was in order. Piper had to tell someone. She needed some kind of encouragement that she was making the right decision. Who better than her fiancé?

By the time she finished dressing and primping, the clock read six thirty. Her bold confession to Rusty would need to wait until after her art rendezvous with Jan and Shep. She was tempted to call him from the car, but then thought better of it. This was not a ten minute conversation to be had while in transit. The two needed to be alone without any distractions. She needed to gauge his reaction so that she could figure out if it was even worth pursuing this gutsy plan. The ramifications were immense. As for Penelope, Piper thought it best to avoid her at all costs. Her little sis had a knack for knowing when she was lying. Piper bit her nails as she drove along. Despite thinking everything through, the fear of making such a monumental mistake got the better of her.

When Piper turned the corner onto Main Street, she took a couple deep breaths to center herself. Something useful she had learned from taking yoga for many years. A parking spot opened up in front of the gallery, which Piper took as a good sign. Sure enough, Jan was seated on a wooden bench waiting for her fellow board member as expected. Jan gave a little wave and stood up to greet her. Since it was after five o'clock, Piper wouldn't need to insert any change into the parking meter. Good thing since Jan seemed eager to see her.

Piper was barely out of the car before Jan started flapping her tongue about it being their civic duty to promote up and coming artists. Piper swallowed hard and prepared for the never-ending lecture. The woman rattled off some names and price points that she wanted them to keep in mind, all the while invading Piper's personal space. Piper pressed on towards the front door deliberately trying to create some space between the two. Jan read aloud some specifics scribbled on a scrap of paper while inching towards Piper. She was so caught up in her chatter that the woman didn't even realize she was suffocating Piper with her close proximity. Magically, Shep appeared holding open the front door welcoming them into his gallery. Piper practically threw herself across the threshold just to get away from Jan.

Shep didn't seem to notice the tension. He jumped right in thanking the pair for coming out on such short notice. "I have a new employee starting tomorrow, a charming young woman named Penelope. I want to have this place in tip top shape before she starts." A broad smile adorned his near perfection face.

Piper flinched when hearing her sister's name mentioned. What she should have said in reply was something along the lines of how much her sister was looking forward to her new position. Instead, she chose to deny her sister for the third time. The obvious biblical reference wasn't lost on her. An onslaught of guilty feelings rained down on her.

Jan took the lead for the meeting. Shep, being an affable gay man, allowed her to take charge. Brandt's collection of paintings wowed even Piper who didn't know the first thing about art. Her only experience with art involved the creation of paint-by-number masterpieces. Coincidentally, she and her sister spent many rainy summer days side by side sitting in front of their easels. Given the circumstances, the memory gave her a momentary pang of guilt.

When it came time to get down to business, the trio squeezed into a small work space located in the rear of the showroom. The area was sparsely furnished with only a white utilitarian table with matching folding chairs. Jan sat down first and made herself right at home. She pulled out some paperwork from her gigantic purse and handed each of them an agenda that she had obviously prepared ahead of time. Piper took a seat and then retrieved a pink moleskin notebook from her purse that she always carried with her. This handy pad contained everything from inspirational quotes to favorite nail polish colors of celebrities. Shep removed his iPad from its sleeve and gently placed it on the table in front of him and proceeded to join them. From the looks of things he appeared to be kind of a trendy dude who kept up with the latest gadgets and apps. All three were prepared for business in their preferred methods of operation.

"Shep, I thought it best to prepare an agenda in an effort to save time," Jan began.

The gallery owner folded his leg across his lap and then hung his right arm across the back of the adjacent chair. "I appreciate you lovely ladies stopping by tonight. As I'm sure you can imagine I'm feeling rather numb these days. Losing Brandt so suddenly and then having to shoulder all the responsibilities for running this place has been overwhelming. I lost a partner in life," he sniffled, "and in business. Brandt was the brains behind this all. I was just the pretty face." He pushed his golden locks out of his eyes. "This library event couldn't have come at a better time. I need something to take my mind off of him. I want to prove to myself that I have what it takes to be successful."

Jan leaned across the table and patted his hand. "There, There. When one door closes, another one opens. I'm sure Brandt is smiling down at you now and encouraging you to take the next step in your life. Don't you worry! Together, we'll make this library ball an evening to remember. Your gallery will become the talk of the town."

While Jan busied herself with playing the role of grief counselor to Brandt, Piper's thumbs were getting a workout under the table. Jay poked and prodded her for an update while she flatly denied having any news.

"Piper?" said Jan. "Did you hear what I just said?"

Piper slipped her phone back into her purse and quipped, "I'm sorry. Would you mind repeating yourself?"

Jan replied, "I said I think it would be best if Shep and I handle the selection of artwork tomorrow morning when his new assistant starts."

"No!" Piper shouted. "I mean, no one should have that much responsibility on the first day."

Jan gave Piper a quizzical stare. "Why's that, Piper?"

Shep cocked his head waiting for Piper's reply.

Piper fidgeted. Speaking with both hands she said, "You see, starting a new job can be very stressful."

"You don't say…" Shep inquired.

Piper jumped right back in. "Yes! I've had my fair share of jobs."

Jan eyed Shep and said, "That much is true. Let's just say her résumé is quite peppered with various employment opportunities."

Piper let the subtle dig slide. "Right. Whatever. So, why don't we get to work now? That way tomorrow, you can devote all your time to training your new employee." She jumped out of her seat. "Jan, how many paintings do we need for the gala? Ten? Twenty?" With a pencil in one hand and her pink notebook in the other, Piper was prepared to get down to business.

Despite being a handsome man, Shep's droopy eyelids showed obvious signs of sleep deprivation. Piper bobbed her head up and down trying to convince

Shep to go along with her suggestion. The weary soul acquiesced. He moseyed out of his chair and shuffled his tired feet towards the showroom. With Piper nipping at his heels, the two left Jan behind contemplating what on earth had just happened.

Shep began their tour with a brief explanation of the gallery. He told them that an eclectic array of artwork hung in the well-lit showroom. The prominent paintings were showcased near the front windows of the store so pedestrians strolling by could stop and admire the remarkable art work. From landscapes to portraits, the gallery procured many significant works of art from well-known artists and local favorites. Sales had been steady since they opened their doors less than a year ago. Now with Brandt gone, Shep wondered about the future.

Piper soaked everything in. "Your shop is truly breathtaking. Kudos to you and Brandt for having the courage to risk your financial security in order to start this small business."

Shep's demeanor changed upon the mentioning of finances. "Oh, Brandt fronted the money for the gallery. Not me. I was just along for the ride."

Piper's eyes popped open in astonishment. *If Brandt was the moneybags behind this operation, what happens now that he is dead?* she thought. Piper didn't have to wait long to find out. Jan took care of the dirty work.

"So, did you inherit the entire business?" Jan made no bones about it.

Piper gasped and then tried to cover it up by placing her hand over her mouth. Only Jan would have the chutzpah to ask such a personal question to a grieving man.

Shep hesitated and then said, "Yes. I will be the sole owner once the estate is settled."

"Wow! Lucky you!" Piper blurted out without realizing she'd said it aloud.

Jan spoke up, "I think Piper meant to say it's quite fortuitous that you will be able to carry on Brandt's vision now that he's no longer with us." Her condescending tone registered loud and clear with Piper.

"It's getting late," Shep announce. "Do you mind if we get to work?"

Both ladies magnanimously agreed.

In an effort to speed up the process, Shep suggested Piper and Jan select ten to fifteen paintings keeping in mind the price point and the clientele that would be attending the event. He would then take into consideration their suggestions to finalize the list of artwork that would be on display at the event.

As Piper flitted around the gallery writing down her recommendations, she noticed Jan and Shep whispering in low voices. Rather than interrupt their private dialogue, she tiptoed behind the partition to listen in without their knowing.

"So, have you given any more thought to the percentage split of the sales? 80/20 perhaps?" Jan inquired.

Shep replied, "You'll have to take that up with Larry. He and Brandt went back and forth with the numbers. I really have no idea what they finally agreed upon. Maybe Piper would know?"

Jan quipped, "No. That's out of the question. As the newly appointed treasurer, she isn't up to speed yet. Regardless, Piper will only be privy to certain financial information like petty expenditures and whatnot, not something as consequential as this. Larry keeps a tight grip on the purse strings. "

Shep brushed over her comments. "Ok. Well, then you might want to get with Larry tomorrow and figure it out. On second thought, leave that to me. Now that I'm the boss, I'll speak with him. I don't need for you to intercede on my behalf. I know how to work him over. "

Piper celebrated Shep's willingness to take charge with a silent happy dance. As for Jan, Piper would deal with her snide remarks later. She scooted out from behind the partition into plain view. "Oh, there you two are." She cocked her eyebrow at Jan.

Jan fumbled for words. "Hi. Um, are you finished? Did you make some picks? Shep and I were just...,"

"Strategizing," Piper finished Jan's sentence. A devilish smirk graced her face.

Jan adjusted her scarf. "Something like that..." she lowered her head. Guilty as charged.

"I think we're through here," Piper announced. She turned her attention towards Shep.

"It has been an absolute pleasure meeting you." The two embraced in a polite hug.

Shep continued, "Perhaps tomorrow my new assistant and I can review your recommendations and then compile the final list."

"Perfect!" Piper nodded her head.

"Next, we'll need to coordinate the delivery schedule. Oh, I almost forgot," said Shep. "I'll need a copy of your proof of insurance for my files just in case one of the paintings gets lost or damaged in transit. It's a customary request when paintings are loaned out for affairs."

Jan inserted herself into the conversation. "I'll take care of that first thing in the morning. Mrs. B. will be the one to provide that information. Anything else?"

"I'll be happy to speak with both Judge Halbreath and Larry in the morning in reference to our negotiated split of the profits. As treasurer of the board of trustees, it's my fiduciary responsibility to oversee all things financial from this point forward." Piper was on a roll. "Furthermore, the board will need to approve our agreed upon amount, so it only makes sense to get Denise involved at this juncture."

Jan remarked, *"Fine.* You do that." Her annoyance with Piper rang loud and clear.

Piper said her goodbyes as did Jan and then the two exited the gallery.

Standing side by side at the curb, Jan said, "Have you met the associate director?"

Piper thought for a moment. "I don't think so. Have I?" She couldn't remember.

Jan cocked her eyebrow. "You have not."

"Is there a reason why?" Piper asked. An incoming text distracted her from the conversation. She fumbled around in her purse in search of her smartphone and keys.

"That's because there is no associate director." Jan announced.

"Good to know." Piper was losing patience with her fellow board member. She jingled the car keys in her hand in an attempt to put an end to the night.

"We don't have one because Larry doesn't want one. He's the sole ruler over the library kingdom," Jan proclaimed.

That bizarre comment grabbed Piper's attention. "I didn't realize Larry is an absolute ruler." She tried to make light of the comment.

Jan lowered her voice to a whisper. "Tread lightly, my friend. Larry calls the shots around here, not Judge Halbreath. You don't want to get on his bad side. It never ends well. I'll speak with you tomorrow. Good evening."

Piper's jaw hung open, but no words escaped. Standing under the street lamp, she observed the innumerable sights and sounds of nightfall as Jan slowly faded away into the darkness.

Chapter 9
Director's Report

Popularity or notoriety equated to success in the work place in Larry's warped mind. As long as there were demands on his time, he believed his job would remain secure. This he had shared with Piper at the beginning of her tenure on the board. The peculiar goings-on as of late reinforced his theory as the man paraded through the library on a daily basis like he owned the place. His employees questioned his unorthodox methods while his board of trustees disregarded his ideas as superfluous. Yet surprisingly, he continued to rule the roost with neither a revolt from his minions nor a slap on the hand from his superiors. Perhaps indeed, Larry outsmarted them all.

Piper arrived at the library promptly at opening time. Calling ahead to check on Larry's availability for the morning with Mrs. B. would have garnered too many questions or opportunities for him to skirt the proposed meeting. The library teemed with patrons in search of the latest book and movie releases. Even the computers were taken at the early hour by senior citizens and college-aged students alike.

Rather than march down the hall to Larry's office demanding his time, Piper tried a more subtle approach. She propped herself up in a study carrel near the main flow of foot traffic and sat in waiting. It didn't take long for her intended target to surface. In true Larry fashion, his attire matched his eccentric personality. A tweed sport coat paired with pinstripe suit pants was his look of the day. The faded blue oxford he wore did little to pull the look together. Just as he was about to pass her area, Piper stood up and purposely bumped into him.

"Piper," he shouted. "Pardon me." He grabbed her by the shoulders to right himself. "For such a petite figure, you took the wind out of my sails."

Piper replied, "I didn't mean to steer you off course." She couldn't help the play on words. "Do you have a few minutes?"

Larry scratched his head, causing his comb over to move off kilter. "I suppose."

Piper hooked her arm into his and together they headed back to his office. Mrs. B. peered over the rim of her bifocals as the two scooted by. She was unable to greet them properly for she was busy attending to a personnel issue over the phone. Larry plopped his disheveled self into his desk chair. Piper sat across from him with her legs primly crossed. She wasted no time getting down to business.

"So, here's the deal. Jan and I met with Shep Stewart last night to handpick the paintings for the ball." She paused to get a read on him. The man sat there stone-faced, not even acknowledging what she'd said. So, she pressed on, "He mentioned the need for us to confirm the split. Since this is my first rodeo, so to speak, as treasurer, I wanted to get your input."

Larry sat up a little straighter, rubbed his chin, and then offered up his best advice, "90/10." He nodded vigorously. "Yes, that's what I'd tell him."

Piper countered, "80/20."

"No, no, no," he disputed. "Shep will never go for that. 90/10 is more than fair."

"Lar-r-y," Piper pleaded with him. "Leave this one to me. I will check in with Brandt..."

Larry's eyes popped open wide at the mentioning of Brandt's name.

Piper covered her mouth. "Oops? Did I say Brandt? I meant Shep. My apologies." She hit a raw nerve, a calculated move on her point. She watched as Larry toyed with a rubber band while refusing to make eye contact with her. A sign that perhaps indicated an underlying meaning which Piper would need to address, but not now. Sensing his anxiety, she rapidly switched gears. "You know what? We're scheduled to meet with Chuck tonight for my orientation. How about if we just do it now instead? We both know Chuck wouldn't mind. Heck, he'd probably prefer it. What do you say?" She double tapped her fingernails on the desk to grab his attention.

Larry stood up. "I think we should stick with our original plan."

Piper didn't let up that easily. "And, why is that? From what I've been told, you're the brains behind this operation. There's nothing that goes on in this library that you don't know about. I'd much rather get my information straight from the premier source. C'mon, Larry. Impress me with your wisdom."

"Well, if you put it that way," he acquiesced.

A little stroking of his ego did the trick.

For the next thirty-five minutes, Larry did almost all of the talking. Piper jotted down copious notes putting asterisks next to things she thought needed further explanation. He glossed over the section concerning the Friends of the library, which came as no surprise. Piper planned on circling back after he finished with his presentation. Mrs. B. interrupted once to get his signature on a couple of documents. She seemed surprised the two of them were taking so long and said as much. Larry didn't seem to mind. Just as he was beginning to wrap up his little talk, his cell phone rang. He took it out of his pocket and looked at the screen. Evidently, he didn't like what he saw. Larry clicked the ringer off and chucked it into the top drawer of his desk.

"Wrong number?" Piper said.

"Yes, yes!" His answer came a little too quickly to be convincing. "Another telemarketer." He gave her an awkward smile.

Mrs. B. barged into his office without knocking. "Excuse me, Larry. Is your cell phone on silent again?"

"No," he removed the phone from his desk drawer and double-checked the ringer. He then looked over at Piper and scrunched up his shoulders.

"Then why didn't you answer it? Nancy is holding on the office line. She said she tried to get you on your cell phone, but it clicked over to voicemail. She needs to talk to you pronto about some report. She says you'd know exactly what she was referring to. She has another meeting in ten minutes, so she doesn't have much time. Pick up on line two, please. Can't you see the light is flashing? You should know by now, mister. It's rude to keep a lady waiting. Sheesh!" She turned around and marched right back to her desk.

Piper couldn't believe her good fortune. No doubt Nancy had some good scoop to share, hopefully pertaining to the missing funds. "Don't mind me, Larry," she flicked her wrist for emphasis. "You go ahead and take that call. I'll review my notes until you're finished. I have nowhere to be but here with you."

Larry insisted, "I don't want to be rude, Piper. I can take this call later."

Piper got up. "Really. I don't mind at all. You mustn't keep Nancy waiting. You heard Mrs. B. It's important." She stepped over the threshold and took a seat in a vacant chair right outside his office.

Larry adjusted the collar of his shirt. "Is it hot in here?" he asked no one in particular. He opened the window a crack to let some fresh air into the cramped space. He sat back down and reluctantly picked up the phone. "Hello?"

Piper's ear was practically plastered to the doorframe. She inched her chair closer trying to catch bits and pieces of their hushed conversation. Just when she thought it was getting to the juicy part, Mrs. B. struck up a conversation.

"So, Piper, how are the wedding plans going? Have you and Rusty set a date yet?"

Piper tried to listen to both conversations at the same time. "Yes, we have. December twenty-eighth."

"Really? That's an interesting choice. Does that date have any significance to you as a couple?" Mrs. B. propped her elbow on her desk and rested her chin on her fist. It appeared as if she was in it for the long haul. "Most couples these days prefer to get married at exotic locales. I think they call that a destination wedding. I guess that doesn't interest you? Do you prefer colder weather? You know, it gets chilly here in Ohio in December."

Piper filtered out as much of the conversation as possible without losing the gist of what the woman was saying. All the while, she heard Larry mention something about verifying the accounts payable. Also, he said something about a loan or paying someone back. She had to strain to hear him speak.

"Piper? So what do you think?" Mrs. B. asked.

Piper forced a smile, "I think getting married around the holidays will be extra special. It's my favorite time of year. Rusty's, too. We already booked the golf club for the reception. Imagine how pretty the course will look covered in a blanket of snow." She didn't wait for the woman to respond. Instead, she got up and stepped closer to the doorway.

"Oh, Piper. You'll look like a beautiful snow princess in your white gown. Have you said yes to the dress? I can definitely see you in something like a fit and flair. Lots of tulle. Maybe crystal appliqués. How do you feel about lace?" Mrs. B. was full of questions.

"Piper," Larry interrupted. "I'm finished with my call. C'mon back in."

Sadly, she had to cut short her conversation with Mrs. B. "Sorry! We'll talk soon," Piper promised.

For the remainder of the morning, Larry gave Piper the low-down on the ins and outs of the library's financial affairs. At one point during their conversation, he did mention something about the Friends group book sales, but when Piper tried to press him on the issue, he refused to engage. Instead, he segued into a brief discussion concerning the ticket sales for the ball and how the members of the Friends group were instrumental in promoting the event. Piper let it slide, for the sheer fact that she didn't want Larry to feel threatened by her nosiness.

Interestingly enough, at the end of their talk, he asked about Penelope, which threw Piper for a loop. Had they met before Penelope was seen near his office on the day of Brandt's murder? She hadn't realized the two were acquaintances. His mentioning her sister's name in passing was just another reason why Piper needed to get with Rusty. She needed help figuring out what was truly going on with Penelope. Not to mention, she'd been running around like a crazy woman for the past couple of days. She needed a Rusty fix. Before she left, Piper made sure to thank Larry for his genuine concern and support through this transitional time.

Once inside her car, she called Rusty and made plans to meet at the coffee shop for a quick afternoon pick-me-up. Rusty warned her that he could only spare about thirty minutes or so because he was in the middle of inventory. He informed her that his Dollar Day sale was coming up, a favorite of his regulars. The opportunity to buy beer or liquor for just a buck over invoice attracted folks from most of the neighboring counties. This sale was the talk of the town.

When Piper pulled into the parking lot, she noticed a familiar looking black sedan parked alongside the entrance. The fish and cross bumper sticker belonged to the hottest bachelor in town, Reverend Black. Since Rusty's truck was nowhere to be seen, Piper thought this was probably a good time to talk to the reverend about her wedding plans. The reception had been booked, but she had yet to confirm the time with the church. A slight oversight, to say the least. Even though Rusty grew up in a strict Catholic household, he agreed to be married in a Methodist church. Just as long as the two said 'I do' was his main concern. Figuring out which house of the Lord they prayed in would be decided at a later date.

Sure enough, the strapping bachelor dressed in his customary black suit and white collar was sipping a cup of coffee smack-dab in the middle of the place. There wasn't a vacant table anywhere near him. All the pretty ladies just happened to be in his vicinity hoping for dear life to catch the hot preacher's eye. Piper by-passed the long line and headed straight for Reverend Black's table.

"Mind if I join you?" She pointed to the vacant chair opposite him.

He snatched up the newspaper he'd been reading and answered, "Please do."

Piper couldn't help but notice the angry stares from the single ladies staking out the neighboring tables. In true Piper fashion, she just played dumb and smiled real big in return.

"Whatcha doing here, Piper?" His big warm smile greeted her. No wonder the ladies were drooling. This man had looks and charm. Plus a pipeline to the big man upstairs. What's not to like?

"Rusty and I are meeting here. Our schedules have been so hectic lately…"

"I can only imagine," he added. "It's not every day you find a dead body. Oh, wait a minute, isn't this the third time?"

It was Piper's turn to interrupt, "Who's counting? Anyway, I'm so glad I bumped into you. Rusty and I are getting married in late December, and I was hoping you'd do the honor of marrying us in your church." She rubbed her hands together in anticipation of his answer.

"Of course! I'd be honored. Do you have a specific date in mind?" He removed his phone from the inside pocket of his suit coat.

Piper spoke up. "December twenty-eighth. Preferably in the late afternoon. Three o'clock?"

He checked his calendar. "Consider it done."

"Thank you! Rusty will be so pleased. We really appreciate it." She lightly clapped her hands in celebration.

"Please stop by the church office within the next couple of days. I'll have my secretary put together an informational packet for you concerning the protocol and such for the big day. Once the date gets closer, we'll meet to discuss the particulars for the ceremony." He lifted his cup and was about to take a sip when Piper started to get up. "Wait. Do you have a minute? I have a favor to ask of you."

Piper sat back down. His unusual request piqued her interest. "Well, of course. What can I help you with, Reverend Black?"

He leaned in closer, "Please, call me Stephen."

Piper sat back in her chair and said absolutely nothing. She couldn't figure out if the reverend was coming on to her or if he was just being friendly. So rather than insult the man, she just blurted out, "Um, Rusty will be here in a minute. I probably should get in line. Do you want anything?"

He glanced at his watch. "I have time for another round. Yes, a tall regular coffee would be nice. Thanks!"

Piper grabbed her purse and stood up. "Sure. How would you like that?"

"Black, of course," he replied with a wicked grin on his face.

Piper slapped herself on the head. "Of course. How else, right?" Her nervous giggle did little to hide her uneasiness. Once in line, she texted Rusty asking how soon he'd arrive. As luck would have it, he hadn't left the store yet. A mad rush of customers came in just as he was about to leave. He promised he'd be there in fifteen minutes or less. Piper hoped for once he was early rather than late.

The line moved quickly despite Piper's wishing it wouldn't. When she made it up to the register, she hemmed and hawed over the selections much to the chagrin of the people standing behind her. Those in need of coffee had little patience, especially when indecisive people like Piper dawdled in line. Some unsavory hippie type had a few choice words about the 'dizzy blonde' mucking up the system. Piper ignored him in favor of stalling even longer than necessary. Finally, Piper settled on a decaf mocha latte. Her order was met with a round of applause which Piper actually found refreshing. With a regular black coffee in one hand and her specialty drink in the other, she returned to the table armed and ready for whatever Rev. Black had up his sleeve.

"Splendid." He reached over and grabbed his piping hot java. "That took a while. Usually, the baristas have no trouble keeping up with the orders. I wonder what happened."

Piper shook her head from side to side. "Hmm. No idea."

"Well, anyway. I'm not sure if you knew this or not, but I was asked to emcee the ball." He removed the lid from his drink.

Piper hesitated a moment because she knew what he was saying was so untrue. At the board meeting, she clearly remembered Rev. Black and Larry arguing over who would make the better emcee. Rev. Black used his doting flock as evidence that he knew better than most how to work a room, or church, for that matter to his advantage. Larry woefully conceded and the reverend won hands down. Having a man of cloth lie about such an inconsequential event bothered Piper to no end. Why would he blatantly lie about such a thing?

"Did you decline?" Her question caught him completely off guard.

His tone shifted from friendly to defensive. "What do you mean? Why would I do that?" He tousled his hair and then straightened his collar.

"I would think as a man of God you'd rather take a behind the scenes approach rather than be front and center. Being emcee is much different than preaching from the pulpit every Sunday. You'll need to be flashy and showy. Flirtatious and bold!" Piper laid it all out there.

"I see what you mean; however, I need to use my God-given talents to the best of my ability for the benefit of the library. Our goal is to raise money, and lots of it. I have experience doing just that...*and more.*" Piper was taken aback by the reverend's healthy and robust self-esteem. She was seeing a completely different side of the man she thought she knew.

"So, what does this have to do with me?" Piper cocked her head to the side in questioning.

Reverend Black leaned in closer, "I need help writing the script. I thought perhaps since you have a way with words, you might be willing to help."

Piper didn't reply right away. Different scenarios were percolating in her head as she tried to formulate a quick response. If she volunteered to help, Rev. Black might feel indebted to her. That could come in handy in the near future. She could use some help delving into the library's finances. Having an ally in her back pocket was always a good thing. If she said no, he'd need to reach out to someone else, probably another board member. Likely choices would be Carolyn or January. Chuck or Denise would be out of the question. Having either one of the ladies closer to the reverend than herself probably wouldn't serve her well. So, the best answer would be, "Yes! I'd be happy to assist you."

As they were cross-checking their schedules to book a future writing date, Rusty finally arrived. Piper hurried the reverend along throwing the blame onto Rusty and his tight schedule. Like a good fiancé, Rusty just nodded and smiled throughout the whole rigmarole. Once the man was out the door, Rusty turned the tables on her and began questioning Piper about what had just taken place. A brief rundown got him up to speed in no time. What he wasn't expecting is what she told him next.

"By the way, my sister is the number one suspect in Brandt's murder case, and she was seen near Larry's office, and Larry asked me about her, which means he knows her, but here's the thing...she has no clue that she's even under investigation. If it's not too much trouble, would you mind helping me clear her name before she winds up in jail...and me with her? Neither of us looks good in orange. Truly, this could become a major fashion emergency of epic deportations if we don't figure out who killed Brandt. Please, Rusty, will you help me?" Her big blue eyes begged for understanding.

Chapter 10
Action Items

"Are you kidding me?" Rusty sat across from Piper with his mouth hanging wide open. "How did this happen? And, what makes you think she's going to get kicked out of the country?"

For the next ten minutes, Piper gave him the lowdown on her conversation with Capt. Morgan, aka his step-father. By the time she was through, he just sat there shaking his head in disbelief not only from the circumstances, but also from Piper's habitual misuse of the English language.

"So, have you talked to your sister?" he asked the most logical question.

Piper scowled. "So, here's the thing. I think it's best if we allow this investigation to unfold organically."

Rusty gave her a questioning stare, befuddled by yet another one of her attempts to use a fancy word. "What exactly do you think that means?"

"I don't know. I heard some actor saying that on television the other night while I was watching *C.S.I.* I thought it sounded hip and cool." She smiled real big.

"Piper!" he shouted. "This is your sister's life we're talking about. Not some make-believe television show."

"Shh!" she scolded him. "Keep your voice down. You think I don't know that? That's exactly why I'm asking you for help. I'm in *way* over my head. And by the way, Capt. Morgan said I couldn't tell anybody that he's investigating her. So, mums the word. I did come

up with my own list of three possible persons of
interest."

He paused in anticipation of the forthcoming list.
She said nothing. "Do you mind sharing it?" He tried to
coax it out of her.

"Oh, sorry. I was just admiring that lady's cute top.
Do you mind if I go over there and ask her where she
bought it?" She tried to get up, only to be pushed right
back down into her chair by her frustrated fiancé.

"Focus, Piper," he insisted. His admonishment did
little to bring her back to the topic at hand. Instead, her
envious eyes watched the woman go right out the door.

"Guess I'll never know now," she said sarcastically
under her breath. "Anyway…back to Brandt. I have it
narrowed down to three suspects." She held her fingers
up. "Want to guess who?"

Rusty acquiesced. "Sure. Desiree," he pushed one
finger down. "Larry," he pushed the next. "Or
Reverend Black," he closed her hand.

Piper waved her fist back and forth. "Oh, my, word!
You think the reverend killed Brandt? I just agreed to
help him write the emcee script for the ball. I'm being
played like an instrument of the devil!"

"I don't know about that," he replied. He held both
of her hands. "I just threw his name in for good
measure. Tell me, love. Whodunit?" He lightly kissed
them.

Piper leaned in real close and whispered, "Desiree,
Larry, or January." She kissed him back on his lips.

"January? Why so?" He gently pushed a stray piece
of her blonde hair out of her face.

Piper said, "I don't trust her. That's all."

Rusty glanced at his watch. "Listen, babe. If you
want to get your sister out of trouble, you'll need to
come up with something better than 'I don't trust her.'
That's not gonna fly in a court of law. Trust me."

Piper fiddled with the stir straw from her coffee. "I owe it to Penelope to get her out of this mess. She's helped me a time or two. It's my turn now."

Rusty warned, "Just don't get yourself into trouble while doing it. I've got to get back to the store. I'll call you later when I'm finished." He leaned over and kissed her atop the head. "Love you."

Piper replied, "Love you, too, babe."

The coffee shop was thinning out, so Piper decided to gather up her belongings and head over to see Jay in the newsroom. If nothing else, it would be a welcome distraction from the horrid circumstances in which she found herself presently.

Upon entering the building, Piper escorted herself to the rear of the office without anyone questioning her presence. So much for the security guard stationed at the front desk. Not much seemed to be happening around the office. Some old guy in the corner sat at his desk eating a tuna fish sandwich on rye while drinking a cup of coffee. A young girl hid behind her laptop, most likely checking the day's Twitter feed. When Piper finally approached Jay's office—a luxury afforded to the owner's son—she could see him with his feet propped up on his desk most likely playing Boom Beach on his smartphone. She tiptoed up behind him and yelled "Boo!" into his ear. Just as she'd expected, his phone went flying up in the air. Luckily for both of them, it landed softly in Piper's hands.

"I thought you were taking this job seriously. Looks like nothing is getting accomplished around here today." She handed the phone back to him. "Sorry about that. I couldn't resist." She tousled his hair.

"Slow news day, or is it?" he inquired optimistically.

"Don't get too excited. I just came by to blow off some steam," she told him.

Jay stood up and stretched his arms above his head. "Word on the street is that Capt. Morgan has a suspect in mind. Has Rusty told you anything? I mean, he is the captain's step-son, right?"

Piper wrinkled up her nose.

"Guess that means no?" Jay removed a pack of gum from his pocket.

"I'll take two please." Piper went to grab some gum from him.

He pulled back his hand. "Only if I get a scoop."

Piper answered, "Really? Hand it over." She stuck out her right hand.

Jay willingly obliged. The need for valuable scoop outweighed his desire to tease her any longer.

"So, I have a few theories on the homicide that I would love to run by you, if you're willing to hear me out." Piper sat down in a club chair facing his desk.

Jay rubbed his hands together for good measure. "Hit me, baby doll." He closed the door to his office and sat down beside her. "I'm all ears."

Piper grabbed a piece of scrap paper from the waste basket by the desk. "No paper around here?"

Jay sighed, "My dad decided to go paperless, supposedly to win some green initiative award from the town. Truthfully, he's just trying to save a few bucks. The profit margin keeps shrinking. No one's reading the paper anymore. If people want to get the news, they search the web. It sucks. No job security around here."

"Maybe this will help you sell some papers. Let's figure out who killed Brandt. If we can solve that mystery, folks will be lining up in the streets to buy a copy hot off the press." Piper didn't wait for an answer. With a pencil firmly in her hand, she wrote Reverend Black at the top of the list.

"Isn't it bad karma or something to speak ill of the clergy?" Jay asked.

Piper quipped, "Only if he's dead."

Jay seemed okay with her answer. "So, why do you think he did it?"

Piper twirled the pencil with her shaped fingers. "Originally, I hadn't given him a second thought until Rusty brought up his name. Now I can't get him out of my mind. What do you know about his latest capital campaign? Did he raise enough money to cover his expenses or is the church in debt? That new addition to the church is a monstrosity."

Jay charged, "Piper, he's a prominent man in the community. What exactly are you implying?"

"Nothing quite yet. Do you have any connections in the financial world? Like a banker friend? Loan officer?" Piper interrogated him.

Jay scratched his head. "As a matter of fact, my cousin is a teller at the bank on Main Street. She's as nosy as all get out. Would she be useful?"

"Here's the thing," Piper used her finger as a pointer. "We need someone to access the church's bank accounts to see if their loan is being paid off. If so, are the payments current?" Piper nibbled on her bottom lip.

"Consider it done. I'll stop by my cousin's house early this evening and see what magic I can work with her. What's your gut telling you?" he asked.

"I think there might be an issue with the reverend's collection plate," Piper said. "It may not be overflowing with an abundance of dollar bills like he'd originally hoped. Is he delivering a powerful message to his flock each week? Probably, but let's be honest. The man is charismatic and easy on the eyes. He could get up there and babble on about absolutely nothing and his audience would still be in the pews hanging on every word. The majority of single ladies are in attendance each week in hopes of landing themselves Woodlawn's most eligible bachelor. An inspirational message would just be an added bonus at this point. The bigger question has to do with him meeting his financial needs. Perhaps he needed some quick cash to supplement his income. That could explain why the library is missing funds. Maybe Brandt found out about it and threatened to expose him. There's no telling what could have happened in Larry's office. Let's start our investigation with him. If we come up empty-handed, we'll move on to the next suspect."

Jay agreed. "How about Capt. Morgan? You never answered my question. Do you think he's investigating Rev. Black, too?"

Piper stood up. "I don't have time to keep tabs on that man. He's probably off on some wild goose chase. Hopefully, you'll be successful in digging up some dirt on the reverend. At that point, I'll share this theory of mine with Capt. Morgan. For now, it's just between you and me. Jay, I really appreciate your discretion in this matter. Call me if you learn anything from your cousin. I've got to get going." She grabbed the piece of paper, stuffed it in her purse, and then began walking toward the office door.

"Let me ask you something, Piper, before you take off. What made you start with Rev. Black rather than, say, someone who may have been spotted leaving the scene of the crime?"

Piper halted mid-way through the doorframe. Acid burned up her throat as she clenched her teeth. Slowly, she craned her neck and shot Jay a piercing look. No words were exchanged, but he heard her message loud and clear. Her stone cold stare did little to dissuade him from backing down. He upped her one by raising his eyebrows. And with that, she twisted back around and left his office without saying a word of goodbye.

As Piper made her way out of the building, all she could think of was her poor sister. Her stomach lurched as she replayed what had just happened with Jay in her head. If he was privy to this information, others surely were in the know. With no other option, she climbed into her shiny black car and headed to the police station.

While sitting at a stoplight waiting for it to turn green, her cell phone buzzed alerting her to an incoming text. A quick glance downward revealed a message from Liz Monroe, her boss at The Cardinal Shoppe. Something about a mix up with a special order caused her to make a quick detour to the store.

When Piper pulled into the lot, she recognized a familiar car parked right smack in front of the door. Her gaze was immediately drawn to the vanity license plate screaming for attention—QBEE. With no other available spots, she pulled up alongside the white luxury sedan and parked. Once outside her car, she couldn't help but peer into the neighboring vehicle's window. Sure enough, strewn about in the back seat was an array of party favors, table linens, and such. She had to fight the urge to open up the car door and investigate the assortment herself. Luckily, a regular customer tooted her car horn as she was exiting the premises. Piper waved hello and then proceeded to enter into the store.

Inside, she discovered Carolyn fluttering around the store from one display to the next in search of the tags. With a pencil perched on her left ear as usual, Liz appeared to be scrutinizing an invoice with the help of her chic reading glasses. Stacked in front of her was a pile of clothes sealed in their original plastic bags from the manufacturer. It didn't take long for Piper to figure out what had happened. Due to an unforeseen fluctuation in her weight, Carolyn had probably ordered the wrong sized outfits. The woman's pudgy cheeks gave her secret away. Piper could sense a tension headache settling in. Before her malady had a chance to reach a point of no return, she grabbed two pills from her purse and headed to the break room for a swig of water.

"Piper! Is that you?" Carolyn asked. "You screwed up my order. Again!"

Piper continued to the back of the store and popped her pills. Feeling armed and ready for what lay ahead, she returned to the front of the store with a fake smile plastered on her tired face. As expected, Carolyn was miffed beyond reason. She rattled off some idle threats to Liz which did nothing to faze the classy proprietor. Dealing with angry customers was commonplace when owning a specialty boutique. Piper and Liz exchanged telltale looks without being blatantly rude to their client. Piper glanced at the invoice and then winked at her boss as if saying, 'I'll take it from here.'

"Carolyn, dear. I see these clothes were ordered in the wrong size. My apologies. Do you need them anytime soon?"

"Yes, as a matter of fact, I do!" Carolyn's voice reverberated off the walls of the tiny shop. Other customers looked up to see what all the commotion was about at the checkout counter.

Piper took control of the situation immediately. "Liz, would you mind reordering these cute outfits in the correct size?" In a hushed voice, she continued, "In the meantime, we'd be happy to offer you thirty percent off whatever you'd like to purchase today."

Carolyn backed down, "Well, that seems fair."

Piper guided Carolyn towards a chic display featuring an up and coming designer. As Carolyn perused the adjacent rack, Piper decided to do a little digging. "So, have you heard if Capt. Morgan has come up with any suspects in Brandt's murder case?"

Carolyn replied, "I don't know why he just doesn't save us taxpayers some money and arrest Larry now before he kills someone else."

Piper leaned in closer. "What makes you think Larry killed Brandt?"

"Oh, I thought by now you'd have figured it out." Carolyn shamed her into feeling dumb.

Piper played along. "Why don't you share your theory?"

Carolyn puckered her lips and said, "I never kiss and tell."

The conversation was not going as planned. "Just spit it out, Mary Queen of Sunshine." Piper was losing patience. "Humor me just this once."

Carolyn admired a flowing pink top. "This would look pretty on you, Piper." She held it up against Piper to take a look.

Piper seethed, "C'mon. Spill it! Why would Larry want to kill Brandt?"

Carolyn smiled. "I don't know. You might want to ask your sister."

Chapter 11
Old Business

The common thread sewing the murder scene together was Piper's sister, Penelope. After hearing from Capt. Morgan, Carolyn, and even Jay that her sister could potentially be involved, Piper had no choice but to confront her. She left The Cardinal Shoppe in a hurry and took off towards Main Street. Rather than park directly in front of the art gallery where she could be seen, Piper pulled around back to the staff parking lot. Sure enough, Penelope's white Lexus was sitting there. Piper parked two spots over and lay in wait. Looking at her watch, Piper realized it was almost noon. Knowing her sister well, she anticipated Penelope would be headed out to lunch momentarily. The sisters were not the pack-your-lunch kind of girls.

The church bells tolled, signaling high noon. On cue, Penelope slipped out the back door with her car keys in one hand and, in the other, a familiar-looking chunky designer purse. Just as she was about to get in her car, Piper beeped the car horn. Penelope was all smiles when she realized who was sitting behind the wheel. She locked her car with the remote control and scurried over to greet her older sister.

Penelope jumped in the passenger seat. "Hi, sis! I wasn't expecting to see you. What are you doing here?"

Piper leaned over and kissed her sister on the cheek. For a second, she flashbacked to religion class, remembering her teacher reading the Bible story of Judas Iscariot and Jesus. A sudden coolness overtook her body, making her shiver. "Um, I wanted to check on you. See how your first day of work was going." Piper sheepishly smiled.

Penelope picked up on the weird vibe reverberating in the car. "You could have just texted me."

"How long do you have for lunch?" Piper tried to redirect her attention.

Penelope answered, "Twenty-nine minutes and counting."

"All right. Let's go to the diner for a quick bite. Send Suzy a text with our order so it's waiting for us when we arrive." Piper handed Penelope her cell phone. "And, yes, you may borrow my Vince Camuto bag."

Penelope was tapping away on her sister's phone. "I'm actually doing you a favor. It was collecting dust in the back of your closet. Now you can buy something new to fill the empty space."

Piper smacked her lips. "I said borrow, not keep."

Once inside the restaurant, Suzy flagged them over to the counter where their lunches were prepped and ready to be eaten. Each had half of a tuna fish sandwich, a cup of tomato soup, and a sweet tea. Piper handed Suzy a twenty dollar bill and told her to keep the change. As soon as the two were left alone, Piper began the interrogation.

"So, have you been keeping abreast of the news of Brandt's murder case?" Piper took a bite of her sandwich. She wiped her mouth with a napkin while waiting for her sister to respond.

Penelope said, "Not really. Why? Is there something I should know?" She sipped some cold iced tea.

"No, no," Piper answered a little too quickly to avert suspicion. "I was just wondering what you might have heard, if anything."

Penelope put down her soup spoon and said, "Okay, what's going on? First of all, you've been acting weird the last couple of days. Every time I've tried to talk with you, you're either A. too busy or B. nowhere to be found. Now today, I find you lurking in the parking lot behind the gallery supposedly just stopping by to say hello and treat me to lunch. You look guilty as heck. Who did you sleep with and does Rusty know?"

The look on Piper's face was truly priceless. "Is that what you think this is all about?" Her face turned beet red and perspiration began to gather at her brow.

"Well if it's not about Rusty, then what is it? You look dreadful, Piper. Oh no! You stopped taking your antibiotics before you finished the entire prescription, didn't you? I knew it! How many times do I have to tell you? You can't do that. Finish your lunch and then you're heading straight home to bed, missy." Penelope glanced at her watch. "I have to leave in five minutes or else I'm going to be late. Hurry up and eat. No talking!"

"But..." Piper said.

"No, buts!" Penelope insisted. She gobbled up the last nibble of her sandwich.

Piper had no choice but to follow suit. She managed to clear her plate within the required five minutes despite choking on some soup. Piper tried to be sneaky by mentioning a neutral topic, but she didn't get too far. Penelope cut her off mid-sentence. It became crystal clear she'd have to address the Brandt murder investigation later when her little sister told her to 'talk to the hand' and then 'zip it.' "Seriously, are we twelve?" Piper mumbled under her breath. "I'd expect more refined terminology from an art aficionado wannabe." Penelope countered by accusing Piper of starting it first. Piper taunted her by saying she hadn't. Typical juvenile behavior continued between sparring sisters.

Back inside the car, Piper had to sit through yet another lecture from Penelope on the necessity of taking all of her pills as prescribed by a doctor. Piper then had to pinky-swear that she would take a break to get some rest. Penelope even snatched up Piper's phone and switched it off for good measure. As soon as they arrived at the gallery, Penelope hopped out of Piper's car and ducked inside the building. Piper was never so happy to be rid of her nagging sister.

As far as Piper was concerned, their luncheon was a complete flop. She'd played out the whole scenario in her head as to how she wanted their conversation to go, but somehow, it hadn't happened that way. Feeling tired and deflated, she drove back home to curl up in bed.

At home, Piper checked the medicine bottle to see if she'd taken the prescribed dosage. Sure enough, she had skipped a couple of doses by pure accident. Piper grabbed a clean glass from the dishwasher, poured herself a cold glass of lactose-free milk from the refrigerator, and then swallowed the mammoth-sized pill. The creamy liquid soothed her scratchy throat. A quick glance in the hallway mirror confirmed what her sister had said. Piper looked completely worn out. Slowly, she climbed the staircase to the second floor as if her bedroom was calling her to sleep. She lazily threw off her shoes and climbed right under the fluffy covers without bothering to undress. As her head touched the pillow, the distant sound of the grandfather clock striking the hour signaled Piper to close her droopy eyes. Within minutes, Piper floated away to an afternoon filled with peaceful sleep.

"Piper! Piper! Wake up," shouted a familiar voice.

Piper kept her lids firmly closed. Last time this had happened to her, she was found yards away from a dead body. Piper took a couple of deep breaths hoping it was only a dream. A pair of moist lips kissed her squarely on the mouth. *This is one hot dream,* she thought.

"I know you're awake. I saw your eyelids flutter. C'mon, babe. Open up your eyes. Your sister's in trouble, big time." Rusty pinched her nostrils shut.

Piper swatted him away with her bony arm. "Stop it! I can't breathe. I have a sinus infection, remember?" She tossed the covers aside and sat up. "Now what's this about my sister?" She swung her feet to the floor.

Rusty handed Piper the cell phone. "Well, if you hadn't put your phone on silent, you'd have known by now. You might want to check your texts."

Piper stood up and stretched her arms overhead. With a big yawn, she said, "Did she call and tell you how *horrible* I am for not taking all of my antibiotics? I hate to admit it, but for once she was right. That was really dumb." She glanced down at her phone. "Holy macaroni! Why didn't you tell me she was at the police station? C'mon! You can fill me in on the way."

Piper threw her shoes on, grabbed her purse, and took off down the staircase. At the bottom of the steps, she tried her best to avert Ralph Lauren who sat ceremoniously in wait, but she squashed the tip of his tail with her foot. A mistake she would definitely pay for ten times over when she returned.

During the car ride over, Rusty filled Piper in on the little that he did know. Thankfully, Capt. Morgan had alerted him to the fact that Penelope had been brought down to the station for some routine questioning. So far, she hadn't been formally charged with anything. Of course, that was subject to change since she'd been there for close to forty-five minutes already. Depending on what she had revealed, the circumstances could have changed drastically.

When they arrived at the police station, Piper spotted a few media people lying in wait with cameras fully equipped with long distance lenses. Before Rusty had a chance to park his truck, Penelope came barreling out of the front door of the building using Piper's ginormous purse to block the camera's view of her face.

"There she is! Look! She's headed to the right side of the building. Drive around there!" Piper feverishly tapped Rusty's arm.

Rusty pulled up alongside the walkway and honked his horn alerting Penelope to their proximity. Penelope peered over the purse and immediately recognized the truck. She made a beeline for the vehicle all the while keeping her head down low. Piper threw the door open wide and proceeded to scooch over next to Rusty to make room for her sister. Penelope jumped in and pulled the door shut. Rusty slammed the truck into gear and proceeded to peel out of the parking lot, leaving the folks from the media covered in a cloud of dust.

"Wow! That was crazy!" Piper shouted. Before she could say anything else, Penelope cut her off.

"Be quiet!" Her voice seethed with anger. Penelope wiggled her back up against the door so that she could look Piper straight in the eyes. "When were you going to tell me that his step-dad thinks I killed Brandt?" She pointed at Rusty.

Piper grabbed hold of Rusty's right arm. "We tried…"

"Are you kidding me?" Penelope clamped her hands on the top of her head out of pure frustration. "Take me home. Now!" she demanded.

Piper wanted to diffuse the situation. "I can understand that you're feeling a little frustrated with Rusty and me right now."

Penelope let loose. "Frustrated? Piper, I'm totally ticked off with the both of you! How the heck did you let it get this far? You're my big sister, for goodness sakes. What happened to sisterly love here? I thought you were supposed to have my back."

Rusty let her finish ranting before he added his two cents. "Look on the bright side. At least Capt. Morgan didn't arrest you, right? That would have been a much worse situation than the one you're in, Penelope. Piper told me you don't look so good in orange."

"Is he for real or what?" Penelope asked her sister.

Piper placed her arm around Rusty's shoulder in a sign of support for her man. "C'mon, Peeps. He was only trying to be helpful here. I know you probably don't want to hear this, but you're the one who has some explaining to do. Why were you at the library around the time Brandt was murdered?"

Penelope sighed. "Like I told Capt. Morgan, Brandt called me earlier that morning and asked me to meet him there. He said he had to drop off some paperwork for Larry and that it wouldn't take but a minute. Since I am not as well versed in art as Brandt would like for me to be, he wanted to help me find some library books so that I could learn more about it."

Piper continued, "So did you meet him?"

"No," she answered. "I was running behind. Since I don't know what kind of car he drives, I couldn't figure out if he was there or not. I ran into the building and the place was mobbed with moms and tots for storytime. I walked around a bit, but I couldn't find him, so I assumed he'd left."

Rusty asked, "So, why didn't you ask one of the librarians if he was there? That would have been the logical thing to do." He pulled the car into Piper's driveway.

"Well I would have, Mr. Know-It-All, if there had been someone available. The checkout line wrapped around the roped-off area and the help desk was three or so deep with patrons. I even walked over to the children's area, but Mrs. Johnson was trying to explain to some poor young mother that siblings were not permitted in the storytime room. Needless to say, the sleep-deprived woman was not taking the news too well. So, I just left."

Rusty turned off the car's engine, but none of them moved. "Did you walk back to Larry's office?"

"I thought about it, but the hallway was crowded with moms waiting to use the family restroom. Like I told Capt. Morgan, I figured he'd already left. I was easily ten minutes late." Penelope rested her case.

Piper could sense that her sister was feeling antsy with the onslaught of questions. But, she needed to ask her just one more thing. "By any chance, did you happen to see one of my fellow board members milling around Larry's office area or even the hallway?"

Penelope paused for a moment and then said, "I'm not really sure who's on the board with you, Piper, except for Judge Halbreath and Carolyn. Oh, I did see Mrs. B., the secretary. It's hard not to miss her with that beehive hairdo she's got going on. She was buzzing around the place."

"That's nothing out of the ordinary," Piper conceded. "She's the one who found me lying unconscious on the floor."

Realizing her sister's presence in the library was nothing abnormal, Piper suggested they all come inside for a late afternoon cocktail.

The three of them assembled in Piper's living room with cocktails in hand clearly was déjà vu. Perhaps strategizing for the third time over potential suspects in a murder case would be the charm. First, it was Charles, Piper's late husband, then poor Congressman Barnes, and now Brandt. Death seemed to transpire in sets of three. For such a small town, Woodlawn did have its fair share of bad luck.

Penelope made herself comfortable by relaxing on the chaise lounge situated close to the fireplace. Rather than soil the fabric with her shoes, she tossed them one by one on the floor close to where Piper was seated.

Piper perked right up when she realized the shoes, too, were a borrowed commodity. She made a mental note to have a lock installed on her closet door at her earliest convenience, a simple act of prudence that would serve her well. Piper didn't mind sharing an occasional item or two for a special event; however, she wasn't willing to lend out her wares on a regular basis.

Confused by the unusual silence between the Chatty Cathy sisters, Rusty struck up a conversation. "Now that we've cleared the air, have you two given any more thought as to who might be responsible for Brandt's death?" He followed up with a swig of beer.

Penelope volunteered her opinion. "I'm not sure, but what I do know is that his partner Shep is one hot mess. That man is riding an emotional roller coaster. One minute he's all business professional making plans for the gallery's future. The next, he's all weepy-eyed, bemoaning the fact that he and Brandt will never get the chance to be married. Did you know they were planning their wedding for this coming summer? He said something about a destination wedding. So sad, if you ask me."

Piper said, "I had no idea. That really is unfortunate for both of them. On another note, I know today was your first day and all, but by any chance were you able to look at their financials?"

"No, but tomorrow, Shep said he's going to start training me on the computer so that I can take over entering the invoices," Penelope answered. "So, I'm assuming he'll be giving me the passwords to the gallery's computer accounts. Give me a few days and I'll report back on what I find. In the meantime, there's got to be someone else you can think of who might have wanted Brandt dead, as morbid as that sounds. C'mon, Piper. Who on the board had it in for him?"

"Better yet, who did he confide in?" Rusty asked.

Piper responded, "I know he and Judge Halbreath were tight. Maybe I should send her a text and see if she's available to meet. Who knows? She may have been privy to his mental state before he died. We don't know if he was sent any threatening letters or email. It's worth a shot."

Rusty rubbed Ralph Lauren's head as he strolled by. The cat retaliated by taking a swipe at him. "Do you think this cat will ever warm up to me?"

The sisters responded together, "No."

"That's what I thought." Rusty watched the little bugger slink away under the couch.

Piper cleared the clutter off the coffee table and then propped her feet up in front of her. "There's also someone named Nancy who's president of the Friends group. Remember when I told you both about the missing library funds?"

Penelope and Rusty feigned no knowledge of the situation.

"Oh, well I thought I did. Maybe I told someone else. Anyway, there's like ten thousand dollars missing from the used book sales and fundraisers from this fiscal year. Larry and this Nancy person were looking into it."

"Bingo! There's your lead. Forget Judge Halbreath. If Brandt was receiving threats, we'd have heard about it by now. Heck, Jay would have splashed that all over the front page of the paper." Rusty revved up his engine. "No, your best bet is hooking up with this Nancy person and finding out what she and Larry are hiding."

"Easy peasy!" Piper liked where this was headed. "I am the treasurer. I'll summon her to a meeting."

"There you go, babe. Throw around your authority. Make her report to you!" Rusty had his guns blazing by now.

Neither Rusty nor Piper noticed that Penelope had left the room until they heard some commotion in the kitchen. The pair got up to investigate the source of the noise. Standing in the middle of the room, they spotted Penelope with an espresso machine in one hand and a Panini press in the other. Strewn all over the floor was a parade of K cups.

Having been caught, Penelope asked, "Mind if I borrow these items? I promise to return them."

Piper replied with a definitive, "No!"

Chapter 12
New Business

The arrival of nightfall signaled Piper's need to get ready. A special board meeting had been called by Judge Halbreath for seven thirty in the library's conference room. Luckily for her, Mrs. B. had sent out a text late in the afternoon to remind all of the trustees. Good thing since it had completely slipped Piper's mind. She was truly impressed with Mrs. B.'s tech savvy skills, especially for someone so advanced in her years. Piper often wondered about Mrs. B.'s personal history. The woman kept her life private, which Piper had a hard time relating to since she was an open book for all to read. If Piper had to guess, she figured Mrs. B. must be close to retirement age. If she were in the old woman's shoes, she'd be on a porch somewhere in the islands with a cocktail in hand rather than stuck in the middle of cornfields in Ohio. Not that anyone had asked her opinion.

Piper debated between wearing flattering dress slacks or a patterned pencil skirt, rather than going with her perfunctory high power suit. Most of the time, she was way overdressed for the meetings compared to the other ladies. Even her nemesis Carolyn, whose go-to option consisted primarily of a sheath dress and pearls, paled in comparison to Piper. The gluttony of suits in her closet was the product of a series of impulse buys. Being afforded the luxury of dressing up once a month got the best of her. On a recent trip to the outlet malls, however, Piper supplemented her professional wardrobe with some more casual pieces. Tonight's wardrobe selection would lend itself to a more relaxed look since there wouldn't be a public session to contend with or questions from the press. Her proudest moment so far had been seeing her name engraved on a shiny brass placard. Positioned in front of her newly assigned board seat, it had signified a new beginning for this former housewife. Times were a changing, and Piper couldn't be more pleased.

The library branch usually remained open while the board meeting was in session, but that wasn't the case this particular evening. Due to the extenuating circumstances surrounding Brandt's premature death, Larry made the executive decision to bar the doors to ward off any unwelcome visitors. Mrs. Johnson, the no-nonsense librarian who ruled the roost, manned the sliding glass doors, hustling the patrons out of the building as efficiently as her arthritic knees would permit.

While making the trek back to the conference room, the board members said their customary hellos to the staff. As usual, Chuck stopped for a moment to check out the latest audiobooks just in case he'd missed the release of a current bestseller. No such luck this time. Waiting in the boardroom sat Larry, Desiree and Mrs. B. in their assigned seats. All were preoccupied with their phones. Not one of them bothered to look up and greet the board members as they arrived.

Piper breezed by everyone and promptly took her seat at the head of the table alongside Judge Halbreath, Chuck, and Larry. Judge Halbreath discreetly asked Mrs. B. to distribute the agenda. Under the heading of New Business, Piper took note of a couple ambiguous line items to be discussed concerning the ball. Rather than state the issues in black and white, Larry's usual *modus operandi* consisted of wording shrouded in secrecy. While the group read over the outline, Piper couldn't help but take a minute to notice the dichotomy in dress between Mrs. B. and Desiree. One looked like she was headed to church; the other was prepped for a stripper pole. Some things never changed.

Judge Halbreath signified the start of the meeting by striking the gavel. Voices hushed as Mrs. B. performed her routine testing of the sound system. She reminded all present that the meeting was being recorded for future reference should a discrepancy arise in the minutes. Chuck hemmed and hawed while Judge Halbreath ran through the typical procedures including calling for a motion to accept the changes to the agenda. As expected, the meeting ran smoothly up until the introduction of New Business. At that juncture, Chuck sat up a little straighter, Carolyn adjusted her glasses, and Rev. Black put away his Blackberry, which he'd been fiddling with for the better part of the meeting.

"The first topic we need to discuss pertains to an amendment of the budget for the ball. Piper, would you like to explain how you arrived at these proposed numbers?" Judge Halbreath began.

Piper drew a blank. She had no earthly clue how or why there was a need for such an amendment.

"Piper?" Judge Halbreath called her name once again. All eyes were upon Piper waiting for an answer.

"I think it's best if I defer this question to our past treasurer Chuck, seeing as I was not made privy to this recommendation prior to the meeting." She turned her gaze in his direction, yet the man uttered not a word. Rather, he shrugged his shoulders in response. "Well then," Piper continued, "Larry would you like to address this, please?"

Larry shuffled some papers around and then handed a stack to Desiree. "By all means." He stood up.

"Desiree here will be passing around the most recent figures for the ball. You'll see that the committees are over budget by just a slight margin. In my professional opinion, not a major cause for concern since this is our first go-round at organizing an event of such magnitude. Realistically speaking, we need to make room for some trial and error along the way."

Piper interjected, "Larry, what do you project as the ballpark figure the Friends group will be able to contribute from its book sales and fundraisers?" All of a sudden, the room got very quiet. "I would assume you have a hard number in mind."

"Good question," Judge Halbreath added.

Larry tampered with his blatant comb-over to bide some time to think.

"Maybe you could get back to us on that, Larry?" Judge Halbreath threw him a life raft, so to speak.

Larry scratched some notes on a piece of paper. "Yes, that's what I'll do. Let me contact Nancy to see where we stand with those numbers."

Piper saw her window of opportunity open. "As the present treasurer, I would like to be in attendance at that meeting. Please follow-up with me when you have agreed upon a time and date. Thank you."

Larry wilted, similar to a flower baking in the hot, summer heat. "Um, yes. Of course, Piper. I'd be glad to include you." His words were far from sincere.

"Well then, how would the board like to proceed, knowing that we're missing an essential piece of information?" Judge Halbreath was a stickler for following protocol.

Reverend Black was the first to speak up. "Regardless of the amount of money that the Friends group can and is willing to provide, the bottom line is that we need to have the funds available to continue prepping for this event. I make a motion that we grant the committee an additional five thousand dollars for operating costs."

Carolyn responded, "I second it." She adjusted her reading glasses so that she could continue reading the financials Desiree had put forth at the beginning of this dialogue.

Judge Halbreath moved along. "Is there a need for discussion?"

Chuck insisted, "I think we all agree that it's necessary. Let's call for a vote."

The other board members nodded in approval.

"All in favor?" Judge Halbreath asked.

The group unanimously responded, "Aye!"

"Opposed?" she said. No one contested. "The motion has passed."

Mrs. B. noted the results in her handwritten account of the meeting.

"Next item on the agenda pertains to the proposed new computer system. Larry, would you like to address the board?" Judge Halbreath gave him the floor.

Carolyn leaned over to Piper and whispered. "What's wrong with the old one?"

Piper answered, "No clue. This whole meeting is a mystery to me."

Larry signaled for Desiree to join him for the presentation. The entire room watched as he escorted the scantily dressed assistant up to the podium. The men drooled while the women snickered at the mismatched pair.

Piper leaned back in her seat in preparation for the ringside show.

For approximately fifteen minutes, Larry reported on the current status of the library's computer system pointing out every last defect imaginable. He droned on and on about how Woodlawn was technologically behind other library systems in the vicinity and how if we wanted to stay current, we would have to upgrade sooner rather than later. Just when it seemed his little talk would never end, Reverend Black raised his hand to ask a question.

"So, let's cut the nonsense here, Larry. You want to replace the library's computer system. We get it. Where do you plan on finding the funds? Do we have money allocated for such? Did you run the numbers by Piper?" He confronted the issues head-on.

Larry squirmed a bit and then replied, "Yes."

"Yes to which question?" Rev. Black was curt with him.

It was now Piper's turn to get in on the conversation. "Whoa, hang on a minute. I don't remember seeing any numbers. Before we get talking dollars and cents, the bigger question here pertains to the library's current records and files. Will they be transferable?"

At this point, Larry deferred to his sexy sidekick.

"I'm afraid not all of them," Desiree informed the group. "As Larry pointed out, our current operating system is rather antiquated. Some of the files may not be compatible with the new operating system. We'll certainly try our best to transition over as many as possible, but realistically speaking, we will lose some."

Sirens went off in Piper's head. What better way to cover up the mismanagement of funds than to delete them entirely? "That's unacceptable."

January chimed in. "Don't you think you're being a little harsh here, Piper? Look at the overall big picture. By upgrading our system, it will benefit not only the library but our community as a whole. I think it's a splendid idea. I'm all for it."

As soon as the conversation heated up, Chuck jumped right in. "Not so fast, my peace-loving colleague. Everything's not coming up roses here. We need to tighten our purse strings at least until the ball is over. I assume we'll be making a profit of some sort. Larry, you're just like my wife. You're spending money before you even have it. Let's wait until the cash hits our account. Then we'll have a better idea as to what we can afford to budget for this endeavor."

Piper liked what she was hearing. "Agreed. I make a motion that we table this discussion until after the ball."

Surprisingly, Carolyn jumped on board. "I second it."

Piper winked at her friend to express gratitude.

Judge Halbreath took over. "Is there any need for further discussion?"

The group let it be.

"All in favor?" Judge Halbreath asked. She pointed over to Mrs. B. to record the vote.

"Aye," replied all present.

"Opposed?" she inquired.

The room remained silent.

"Thank you for your swift call to action, my fellow board members. Is there any other new business that needs to be brought forth this evening?" Judge Halbreath glanced at the trustees seated around the table. No one spoke up.

"Well then, the meeting is adjourned. Good evening." She tapped the gavel one last time.

Larry's delicate ego had taken quite a brow beating since neither of his proposals made it through to a vote without intense scrutiny. Quietly, he ushered Desiree aside, bypassing the others as they made their way around the table towards the exit. His deliberate maneuver enabled him to skirt additional questions from the board members who lagged behind to engage in casual conversation.

Piper debated whether to intrude on their private talk, but then opted for a more proactive approach by soliciting Mrs. B. for Nancy's contact information. The woman readily provided it off the top of her head and even recommended the best time of day to reach out to her based on Nancy's schedule. Piper reciprocated the kindness by giving Mrs. B. an affectionate hug. Piper's reluctance to leave for fear of missing out on important gossip turned out to be fortuitous as she listened in on an exchange between the two strongest personalities on the board.

"How's that capital campaign going?" Chuck pried into the reverend's business. The two moseyed towards the exit.

"Not as well as I'd hoped. The parishioners' utmost desire to build a state of the art facility doesn't quite match their wallets. No doubt I'll be on the pulpit once again this Sunday begging for additional pledges. The exuberance of the flock wanes as soon as I mention the word money." The reverend shared his woes with his colleague.

Chuck continued, "Well, I wish you the best. Maybe you should pray for a windfall from the heavens above."

Rev. Black chuckled, "You don't know the half of it!" He patted Chuck on the shoulder as the two left the building.

Soon after, the rest of the board followed suit, leaving Mrs. B. and Larry behind to secure the building and lock up. Piper was hoping to catch up with Carolyn to get her take on the situation, but the queen bee of the country club split as soon as the gavel hit the sounding block. Once inside her car, Piper checked through her messages to see if anything important had come up while her phone had been in silent mode. Sure enough, a barrage of texts from Jay lit up the screen begging her for the 411 as soon as the meeting ended. Piper tossed her phone back into her purse and put the car in drive. The only talking she felt like doing involved the sexy man she couldn't wait to marry. Then again, words might not even be necessary.

Soon after, Piper pulled into the liquor store lot where she spotted Rusty standing at the front door waiting to lock up. The final stragglers exited the building content with their brown paper bags filled with booze. Piper flashed the high beams so that he would see her. He waved right back and then held up ten fingers signaling the amount of time he'd need. She doubled flashed her lights to let him know she understood. While in limbo, she decided to check in with Jay after all. She knew he'd be anxious to hear from her. She dialed his number, which sent her directly over to voicemail. As she was leaving a message, the call waiting beeped, letting her know that he was holding on the other line. She ended the call and switched over to talk with him.

"Hey, there," her voice dragged. "From all the text messages you left cluttering up my phone, I'm surprise you didn't pick up on the first ring."

Jay mumbled some random words.

"Try again, my friend. You're breaking up." She chipped away at her gel nail polish as she waited for him to respond.

"I said I was busy getting the scoop about the suspect Capt. Morgan brought in for questioning early tonight," he told her. "The whole town is buzzing."

That caught Piper's attention. "Suspect? Who?"

"Rumor has it the president of the library Friends group, Nancy. She was in the hot seat. What do you know about her?" Jay volleyed back to Piper.

"Not much, except for the fact that she barged into Larry's office to help herself to some files while the hazmat crew was sterilizing the place," Piper volunteered.

"Oh, interesting. Go on," Jay prodded her for more information.

"Um, I think that's about it." Piper clammed right up.

"Piper O'Donnell. Even over the phone I can tell you're lying. Fess up or I'll let it slip that you have a tattoo on your…"

Piper reacted to his crudeness. "You wouldn't dare make up a lie like that."

Jay poked fun at her. "Imagine what the ladies at the club would say. Oh! The horror of it all."

"Jay Baker! Get a hold of yourself. You're just being mean. Knock it off!" Piper scolded him.

"So, as you were saying…" Jay prodded her.

Piper surrendered. "Fine. I have no proof, but I have reason to believe that Nancy and Larry may be involved in a money laundering scandal at the library."

"Wow! That's some accusation, my friend. And how exactly did you arrive at this theory?" Jay grappled with the validity of her bold statement.

"Well, let me explain. There's approximately ten thousand dollars unaccounted for from the Friends' book sales and fundraisers. Seriously? That's a huge chunk of change to go missing. Brandt had instructed Larry to get to the bottom of it *tout de suite*. Of course, that would entail him meeting with Nancy, which he has yet to do. Personally, I think Larry's stalling. Earlier this evening, I requested to be present when the two finally meet face to face, seeing as I'm the new treasurer. My request appeared to have nauseated him. The man turned white as a ghost. No joke."

"Get out of here!" he teased.

"I kid you not. If I didn't know any better, I'd swear the man is deathly afraid of confronting this Nancy woman. Not sure why." Piper took a breather.

"Of course he doesn't want to confront her. The man is wallowing in self-pity. He's already played that game and lost big time," Jay told her.

Now it was Piper's turn to ask the questions. "Hold on a minute. I don't get it. Why in the world would Larry be afraid of Nancy?"

Rather than answer, Jay posed a question. "Piper, do you happen to know Nancy's last name?"

"Funny you should ask that," she replied. "No one at the library seems to remember. Jay, do you know what it is?"

Jay spilled the beans. "Flagstone."

It took a moment for it to sink in. "She's Larry's sister?" Piper enquired.

"Heck, no," Jay replied. "Nancy, my dear, is Larry's ex-wife."

Chapter 13
Business from Chairperson

Piper could barely contain herself when Jay revealed the salacious news concerning Larry and Nancy's previous relationship. She hit him up with a barrage of questions mostly looking for some juicy details surrounding the reason for their split. Like a typical guy, Jay had little to share which greatly disappointed Piper. A call came in from Jay's boss, aka his dad, so he clicked over, leaving Piper hanging on for a few minutes. When he returned to the line, Jay apologized for making her wait and then informed her that duty called. Evidently, the local teachers' union was up in arms over some potential layoffs for the following school year. Jay had been summoned to the council meeting to report on the specific details. His departure was perfectly timed with the arrival of Rusty who'd just approached Piper's car.

Piper started the engine and then hit the automatic button to roll down the driver's side window. Rusty wasted no time sticking his carrot top head inside her car in order to plant a hot kiss on Piper's luscious pink lips. Piper bubbled over with excitement as she began to share a veritable treasure trove of information. Rusty stopped her mid-sentence with another smooch and then sweetly proposed continuing their delicious conversation bedside. Piper pulled him in closer for another peck signifying her approval of his romantic proposition. Soon after, the lovers left the parking lot in their respective cars with their sights set on reaching Piper's cozy lair.

Over the last few days, the couple had not seen much of each other. On the verge of marriage, this lack of togetherness had the potential for becoming the kiss of death. As if reading each other's minds, they shelved their talk about Brandt's murder case for the time being. Instead, Piper grabbed two wine glasses while Rusty selected one of their preferred bottles of wine. The pair walked hand in hand up the grand staircase. When they made it into the bedroom, the two undressed and then slipped between the soft satin sheets. Rusty poured them each a glass of wine to celebrate an evening filled with nothing but love.

Piper woke up around one in the morning. She lingered in bed for a while, but couldn't fall back to sleep. Not wanting to wake Rusty, she slipped out of bed and headed down to the kitchen for a late night snack. As she peered into the refrigerator, she felt a warm bundle of fur brush up against her. Piper chose to ignore her cat's affectionate greeting causing him to meow in protest. Instead, all her attention was focused on a jar of crisp, green kosher pickles resting on the top shelf of the stainless steel refrigerator. Ralph Lauren decided not to compete with her craving and ambled off towards the living room in search of a comfy space for a well-deserved catnap. Piper, on the other hand, helped herself to two plump pickles, one for each hand. She made her way over to the kitchen table, sat down, and savored each crunchy bite.

With her hunger satisfied, Piper unplugged her phone from the charger and meandered into the living room to check Instagram. She spotted Ralph nestled on the corner of the couch and decided to join him. When she reached out to pet him, he swatted at her with his paw. The finicky cat wanted no part of his owner in retaliation for her recent snub in the kitchen. Piper moved aside, giving him all the space he needed. She knew better than irritate a cranky senior cat.

Piper perused her Instagram account to check up on her favorite celebrities. She liked seeing the premieres and after-parties they attended and what new designers were being plugged. In some ways, she felt as if the celebs were real friends. At times, she knew more about them than her own family and friends. Evidently, it had been a slow night. Not too much to report except from the frequent Instagram users—the Kardashian clan.

Rather than stalking the celebrities, Piper initiated a search for information about Nancy Flagstone. The first two entries to pop up were her profiles on LinkedIn and Facebook. Piper initiated contact by requesting to be added to both accounts. She wondered how long it would take for Nancy to respond to her requests. By infiltrating the woman's social media circles, Piper knew she'd be able to get a handle on Nancy's associates and other interests she had besides stuffing cash into her pockets. Next, she clicked on images to get a sense of Nancy's looks and style. Piper was blown away from what she could see. Nancy appeared to have brains, beauty, and business sense. How Nancy got tied up with Larry was a mystery to her.

Piper stifled a yawn as she peered at the clock on the mantle. Having wasted an hour, she decided to drag her tired self from the couch and make her way back upstairs to bed. Sure enough, Rusty rested peacefully on his side, snoring away, not even missing her warm body which should have been snuggled up alongside him in bed. Piper walked into the bathroom to brush her teeth. She wanted to rinse the garlicky taste of the pickles from her mouth before attempting to fall back asleep. She flipped the light switch on for just a second to check her appearance in the mirror. The bags under her eyes did little to help her desired sultry bedroom look. As she tiptoed back to the bed, she accidentally tripped on one of Rusty's shoes causing her to crash land into the bed. Rusty stirred for a moment, but luckily he didn't wake up. Piper climbed under the sheets and listened as the pitter pattering of the rain lulled her into a quiet slumber.

The next morning, Piper stretched out her arm in search of her handsome hunk but came up empty-handed. She lifted her head off the pillow and peered over to his side of the king-sized bed. Sure enough, he was long gone. Piper noticed a sticky note attached to his memory foam pillow. She leaned over and grabbed it without exposing the rest of her body to the cool morning air. His sweet words of endearment were no substitution for his warm body. Rather than wallow in the fact that he was booked for the entire day, Piper decided to be proactive and pay a little visit to Capt. Morgan and his wife, Helen. Despite having failed to get the pertinent information from Jay, she still had recourse to a higher authority. Being engaged to the policeman's step-son had its privileges. Piper quickly dressed, primped, and then ate a blueberry Greek yogurt before stepping out the door.

First on her busy agenda was the mandatory caffeine run to her favorite coffee shop. She needed to be well fueled for this trip. She zipped through the drive-thru in no time flat, benefits of being a regular customer. Next, she ducked into the local bakery for an order of fresh sticky buns—Capt. Morgan's guilty pleasure.

The Morgans lived not far from Piper's house. Often times, she passed them on her way in or out of the neighborhood. Due to the morning school congestion, Piper veered down a side street so that she wouldn't get stuck behind a school bus. As she approached the homestead, she could see Capt. Morgan's squad car still parked in the driveway. Their unassuming house looked well cared for with bursts of color in the flowerbeds and trimmed greens. Piper parked right behind his car to block him in. A captive audience proved to be the best kind in this type of situation.

While juggling her purse, coffee, and bakery treats in her arms, the front door of the residence flew open. Standing in the entry dressed in a red and navy plaid robe, black dress socks, and a ball cap was the man of the hour. At first, he didn't spot Piper. His eyes zeroed in on the wet newspaper spread across his front stoop. He mumbled a few choice words before he caught sight of Piper in his peripheral vision.

"Dang it! My paper is soaking wet. How am I supposed to read it drenched like this?" he griped.

Piper approach the doorstep, "It's that unexpected rain shower we had last night. The weatherman didn't see it coming. Betcha your newspaper carrier didn't either. I brought you some sticky buns for breakfast. Hope you haven't eaten yet." She presented the box to him.

"Awfully nice of you, Piper. What do you want?" He wasn't fooled by her generosity.

Piper guffawed. "Well, are you at least going to invite me in?"

"Do I have to? I could just take these scrumptious buns inside with me and call it a day." His swift parry caught her off-guard.

"Piper? Is that you I hear?" called a voice from inside.

Piper marched up the steps, snatched the box right out of his hands, and proceeded to walk in the house. "Yes, Helen. I brought you a yummy treat." The door slammed shut behind her, leaving Capt. Morgan out in the cold.

Helen was a genial host welcoming Piper into the home and offering to reheat her take-out coffee in the microwave. As Helen rolled herself in the wheelchair over to the waist-high appliance, Piper sat down at the kitchen table. The two chit-chatted about nothing in particular as Piper waited for Capt. Morgan to come storming into the room. On cue, he bolted through the doorway with a stream of expletives escaping from the side of his mouth. Helen reprimanded him for using such foul language in front of Piper and then soothed things over by handing him a plateful of sticky buns. Capt. Morgan chose not to quibble over the fact that a grown man had just been scolded in his own home. He was too busy savoring the sweet taste of the buns to protest. Piper stifled a laugh as she watched him devour the bakery treats one by one.

"Have you seen Rusty? I don't think he ever came home last night. I assume he was with you?" Helen asked. The woman made no bones about the fact that she did not approve of premarital sex. A staunch Catholic, she followed the church's rules despite her son's obvious disregard for her old-fashioned beliefs. Rusty lived in the garage apartment behind the Morgans' home, partly to help out with his mom's physical needs as necessary. Now that she had married Capt. Morgan, he wasn't needed as much anymore.

Piper was in no mood for a lecture, so she sidestepped the issue entirely. "Did you hear the good news? Rusty will be supplying the liquor for the Booklovers' Ball at the library. What a fabulous opportunity for him to drum up business."

Helen peered over the top of her reading glasses. "I imagine you were instrumental in making that happen?"

Piper tried to help herself to a sticky bun but was thwarted by Capt. Morgan's quick reflexes. He closed the lid on the box and placed it on the countertop behind him. Helen didn't interfere seeing as Piper's deliberate omission of info concerning Rusty's whereabouts last night confirmed his participation in risky business. Instead, Helen sat there innocently with her hands folded in her lap waiting for clarification of Rusty's latest venture.

Capt. Morgan scowled, "How much did he commit to give away for free? There's always a catch, Helen."

Piper answered, "He's providing the liquor at a discounted rate in exchange for advertising and future recommendations to other organizations in town."

"He's breaking even," Capt. Morgan clarified.

"He'll come out ahead," Piper explained.

Helen could sense an argument brewing. "So what brings you by?" Smart woman to change the subject.

Piper took the bait. "I heard you had a chat with Nancy Flagstone concerning Brandt's murder case. I find her to be a fascinating woman in her own right. Learn anything?"

Capt. Morgan squelched the chance of any rumors getting started by simply stating, "I can't discuss the case."

"Sure you can. We're family," Piper said.

"Not yet. Rusty still has a chance to change his mind before it's too late."

Helen smacked him on the arm. "Be nice."

Piper added, "You better get used to it because I'm in it for the long haul."

Capt. Morgan rolled his eyes.

"Anyway, since you can't comment," she made quotation marks with her fingers when she mentioned the word *comment*, "then just sit there and listen." Piper divulged everything she knew about Larry, Nancy, and the missing funds, grabbing Capt. Morgan's full attention. She even went so far as to present viable reasons why she believed one or both of them could potentially be culpable of the crime.

Capt. Morgan did not appear eager to respond. He scratched his nose, adjusted his watch, and then drank a big gulp of coffee. Just when Piper was about to lose it, he responded, "I agree."

Piper tried not to agitate him. "Um, with which part?"

"With most of it, but there's no evidence supporting it," he affirmed.

Helen whispered in his ear, "I'm not sure it's prudent to discuss the case at this juncture." She sheepishly smiled at Piper.

Capt. Morgan lightly patted her on the forearm. "I have someone looking into the library's finances as we speak. I'll know soon enough. In the meantime, why don't you concentrate on that ballroom dance party of yours, and I'll take care of the investigation."

"It's Booklovers' Ball," Piper corrected him. She crossed her arms and pouted. Just then, her cell phone rang. A pop song with a catchy beat advised her to shake it off. Sound advice since the conversation appeared to be going nowhere. "Hello," she answered the call.

"Piper, I have some news," Jay informed her.

Piper covered her mouth with her hand. "Hold on a second." She addressed the couple. "I need to take this call in private." She rose from the table.

"Probably another boyfriend of hers," Capt. Morgan snickered.

"No, it's your lady friend from last night." Piper held the phone out to him.

Capt. Morgan's face turned beet red. "That's ridiculous. I swear I was at the diner with Chief Derbyshire." Helen raised her eyebrows in disbelief.

Piper left them alone to bicker as she made her way down the hall to the guest bedroom. With the door closed, she got back on the line. "Okay. I can talk now."

"Stirring up trouble with your in-laws?" he asked.

Piper said, "He deserved it. The man wouldn't share his sticky buns. So, what's going on?"

"It took a while for my cousin and me to sync our schedules, but we did find time to meet. We had coffee this morning," he informed her.

"Oh, that's nice. I'm glad you're keeping in touch with your family." Piper tried to feign interest, but she couldn't figure out why he felt the need to share his news.

"Piper, I'm referring to my cousin who works at the bank. Remember?" he clarified.

She finally clued in to what he was saying. "Oh, yes! Now I know what you're talking about. What did she find out about Reverend Black's church?" She could hardly contain her excitement. "Do tell!"

"You were right!" he announced.

"That shouldn't be news to you, Jay," she chided him.

"Hush! Let me finish. I don't have all day."

Piper said, "Please continue. I'll be quiet now."

"The Woodlawn United Methodist Church is four months behind on its loan payments. Rev. Black's been paying towards the interest, but not the principal."

"Get out!" Piper shouted at the top of her lungs.

"Everything okay in there?" Helen tapped on the bedroom door.

Piper whispered into the phone, "Hold on again." She hurried to the door and cracked it open a bit, "Yes, Helen. I apologize for screaming. Everything's perfectly fine. I'll just be another few minutes or so. Promise."

Satisfied with Piper's response, Helen scooted her wheelchair back towards the galley kitchen.

Piper clicked the door closed. "I'm back."

"Where are you, by the way?" Jay asked.

"I'm at Helen's house. I dropped off some sticky buns like a good future daughter-in-law would do. Capt. Morgan invited me to stay for a while and visit." Her condensed version teetered on the edge of truth, but Jay wasn't buying it.

"Ran the Nancy/Larry/money missing scenario by him, didn't you? He told you to go fly a kite. Am I right?" Jay could read her like a book.

"Something like that," Piper conceded.

"It was worth a shot. I get you. So, what do you think about Reverend Black's financial situation? My cousin said there's no record of him applying for a loan modification. As it stands now, he's negligent on his payments. Without a doubt, the church is in dire straits. But do you think the lack of cash flow would spur him on to take matters into his own hands by pilfering money from the library? How can that be? Stephen Black is a holy man, not a common criminal." Jay presumed.

"I hear what you're saying. He *is* a highly reputable man in our community, but you can't ignore the fact that Rev. Black is a sophisticated schmoozer for lack of a better term. I'm meeting him in an hour at the church to assist him with the emcee script for the Booklovers' Ball. Let me think about how I might be able to tie in a discussion of the church's finances. It's worth a try."

"If anyone could work that angle, it would be you. Good luck, Piper. Don't forget to call me later with the results. I've got to run. Bye!" He hung up.

Piper straightened the covers on the twin bed where she sat and then headed back to the kitchen. The clutter still occupied the table, but no one was in the room.

Piper shouted a couple of times, but all she heard in response was the echo of her own voice. Realizing she'd been abandoned, she reached for her purse. In one last attempt to locate the zany pair, she exited through the back door that led to the garage apartment. Sure enough, she overheard them nitpicking Rusty about his demanding work schedule. Evidently, his full calendar was preventing him from joining his folks for a leisurely lunch. Helen aired a boisterous complaint concerning the fact that she hardly ever saw him anymore due to the liquor store and the landscaping business. Rusty was quick to remind her that those businesses kept a roof over her head during the difficult times. Capt. Morgan remained neutral since he probably preferred the peace and quiet anyway. As Piper approached the group from behind, she waved her arms overhead trying to catch his eye. As soon as she came into view, Rusty rushed over to greet her, effectively cutting short his mother's guilt trip. Both young and old engaged in polite conversation about nothing in particular and then seamlessly parted ways.

Piper discovered that, indeed, Rusty had been true to his word. Duty called him for the day to a neighboring town for a lucrative commercial landscaping job. As he explained to her, these last minute opportunities helped to finance their upcoming honeymoon. Rusty dreamed of escaping to an exotic locale with his blushing bride by his side. Piper giggled as he described in full detail his interpretation of the ideal lovers' getaway. His enthusiasm warmed her heart.

With thirty minutes to spare before her scheduled meeting at the Woodlawn United Methodist Church, Piper decided to drop by the fancy bagel shop on the corner of Main Street and Lockwood Avenue for a homemade fruit smoothie. Too often, she neglected to treat herself to such a healthy indulgence. The yoga studio was located right next door, making the bagel shop a popular destination after class. After parking her vehicle, she strolled down Main Street soaking up the spring sunshine. The sidewalks bustled with pedestrians enjoying the fair weather after having been stuck inside with the recent rainstorms. Once she'd arrived, Piper peered in the window to determine its busyness. The tables were packed with animated patrons enjoying the mid-morning reprieve. Piper decided to give it a go and walked through the revolving doors of the lively establishment.

The line appeared to be moving at a steady clip. Most customers opted for a bagel with a schmear of cream cheese and a cup of coffee. A few ordered smoothies or bagel sandwiches with egg. Piper squinted at the menu mounted on the wall behind the counter hoping to read the tiny print accompanying the names of the various fruit smoothies. Inching closer, she happened to knock into the woman standing directly in front of her.

"Oh, excuse me," Piper proffered.

The skinny woman turned around while saying, "No worries."

"Desiree! Oh, hi! I didn't realize it was you standing there. I was trying to get a better view of the menu. I want to order a smoothie, but I don't know which one to pick." Piper's genuine smile put Desiree at ease.

"My fave is Caribbean Passion. I love the taste of mangoes mixed with sweet peaches."

Piper arched her brow. "Interesting combination! Thanks for the suggestion. I think I might give it a try."

The line stalled for a bit as a mom with three small children debated over which flavors of cream cheese to order with their assortment of bagels. To pass the time, Piper did her best to engage Desiree in small talk. "I see you're dressed in yoga clothes. Did you come from class?"

"No, I'm on my way to the library to meet with Larry. Thought I'd stop by and pick up something to eat. How about you?" She reached her arm across the front of her body stretching out her shoulder blade.

Piper thought twice about sharing the details of her upcoming meeting with Reverend Black. As an alternative to sharing her private affairs, she elected to pry into Desiree's business instead. "Any new developments I need to know about concerning the ball? Oh, and how many tickets have sold?"

Desiree burst with joy as she proudly announced that all the tickets had been sold. She droned on about her instrumental role in making it happen.

Piper stroked her ego just enough to make Desiree think she truly cared. Then, she proceeded to use Desiree to her full advantage. "Tell me what you know about Larry's ex-wife Nancy. You know, the woman in charge of the Friends' group." Her pointed question wiped the smile right from Desiree's face.

"What exactly do you mean?" Desiree stammered.

"I just find it odd that no one has ever mentioned their torrid past or even their connection to one another. Don't you agree?" Piper inched closer, infringing upon Desiree's personal space.

"I can help whoever's next in line," the pimply teenager from behind the counter spoke up too soon.

"That's me." Desiree shuffled up to the counter so as not to lose her turn. "We'll have to catch up another time. Good seeing you, Piper."

"Next!" someone shouted. Piper said goodbye and then hurried over to the far cash register to place her order with the worker.

Piper didn't have an opportunity to grill Desiree any further for when she picked up her order at the counter,

Desiree was long gone. Piper had a gut feeling there was more to Desiree and Larry's meeting than just a perfunctory exchange of information. His current role as director gave her the impression of being a complete farce. January had warned her about the dangers of revolting against the supreme ruler of library land, but from Piper's astute observations, Larry clearly had been serving as a puppet for someone far brighter. Nonetheless, whoever orchestrated the demise of Larry's adversary, Brandt, had yet to be perceived as the villain.

Chapter 14
Business from Board Members

At the stoplight, Piper sucked on the straw from the Caribbean Passion fruit smoothie in order to savor the last few drops of her drink. She had Desiree to thank for recommending such a heavenly pick-me-up. Once the light turned green, she proceeded down the road in search of Church Street. Whoever named the roads in Woodlawn lacked an imagination. One would think the church would be located on the corner, but that wasn't so. Piper crossed over two more intersections before the road dead-ended into the church's miniscule parking lot. Compared to the massive structure situated on the lot, it looked gravely out of proportion.

Due to the time of day, Piper had her pick of parking spots. She eased her car into a primo space located right next to the pastor's designated spot. While exiting her vehicle, she accidentally knocked her car door into the side of Reverend Black's white car. She inspected hers for damage first and noticed no visible markings; however, Rev. Black's Cadillac didn't fare as well. Piper wet her thumb on her tongue and then did her best to rub out the mark. All it did was deposit her saliva on his pristine sports car. Piper surveyed the area for bystanders of which she found none. She then grasped the hem of her shirt and polished the area to remove any sign of her presence. Confident the man wouldn't notice her slight transgression, she proceeded to head towards the buildings.

Affixed to a medium-sized pole rested a site map. Good thing since Piper had no clue where to find Reverend Black's office. She perused the layout in search of some tell-tale sign, but came up empty-handed. Agitated, she reviewed the placard one more time before giving up completely. Instead, she decided to partake of a self-guided tour. Glancing at her watch, she realized her limited time frame would prohibit her from exploring too long. Yet, her daring plan was thwarted by the sudden appearance of the man himself.

"There you are!" he shouted. "I had a feeling you might be lost." He cozied up alongside Piper, placing his muscular arm around her shoulders.

Usually, Piper liked when people greeted her with a hug, but something about a man of the cloth embracing her in such a familiar way felt downright sacrilegious. She took a step back and greeted him with a friendly smile. "Quite the place you have here."

The two walked side by side into the main sanctuary.

Piper drew in her breath upon seeing the majestic altar consecrated inside the structure. "I can only imagine how much money this cost to build."

Rather than respond to her observation, he kept quiet as they walked to the rear of the building. Tucked away behind the grand altar was his office. Seated outside the doors sat his secretary. The young blonde looked barely old enough to be out of high school. Piper introduced herself as Rev. Black's favorite board member, triggering a chuckle from the preacher. As for his actual office, it matched the magnitude of the church. Expensive furniture adorned the room, a masculine desk and chair, a conference table, and two brand new club chairs. The desk was positioned in front of a spectacular window, framed by luxurious custom drapes in vibrant blue hues.

Rev. Black offered her a seat in one of the upholstered club chairs while he gathered up his notes strewn across the desk top. He removed two fancy pens from a Woodlawn United Methodist Church coffee cup and then sat down in the adjacent chair. He handed her a small yellow notepad and a pen.

"Thanks, again, for agreeing to help me with this Herculean task. I have plenty of experience writing up sermons, but to construct an emcee script is out of my comfort zone." He rested his leg across his lap.

Piper was tempted to remind him that no one twisted his arm to do it. He voluntarily accepted the job. "It's not going to be as difficult as you may think. I've emceed many a fashion show for The Cardinal Shoppe. All you need to do is keep the event moving forward. Have you spoken to Shep Stewart at Brandt's gallery?"

"No! Why would I?" he responded a little too forcibly.

His adamant denial confirmed her initial suspicions that perhaps he was involved in some sort of wrongdoing. "Oh, I'm surprised since he's the one who selected the paintings we'll be using for the ball. Correction. He and January finalized the list. Those paintings will fill up a major chunk of your emcee script. Would you like for me to call my sister and ask her to fax it over to you? What's your fax number?"

Reverend Black looked dazed and confused. "I don't understand. How is your sister involved here? Is she on a committee or something?"

Piper laughed. "Oh, no! Suffice it to say my sister is not the committee type. She prefers one on one engagement to a group. Anyhow, Penelope is now working at the gallery alongside Shep. She's training to become the new assistant manager."

He paused for a moment at hearing the news, and then said, "You don't say? Well, I guess congratulations are in order. Good for her."

"Thanks! I'll be sure to pass along your well wishes. Truth be told, it's not going to be as easy of a transition as she'd originally thought. There's quite a learning curve to overcome since she isn't too knowledgeable when it comes to art. Thank goodness she's a financial whiz."

Reverend Black said, "Really?"

"Oh, yes!" Piper affirmed. "I may be biased, but I do believe my sister will prove to be invaluable to Shep in no time. Just between you and me, Brandt saddled Shep with several cases of misappropriated funds. No worries, though. Penelope hungers for a challenge such as this one. Mark my words. It will all be straightened out in no time. You watch."

Beads of perspiration began to form on the preacher's forehead. Piper remained still in anticipation of his next words.

"Perhaps we should reschedule this meeting for another day." He deliberately glanced at his watch. "It slipped my mind. I'm supposed to meet with the choir director to discuss some crucial changes to the music program." He stood up from his chair. "I apologize for having you come all the way over here for me to have to cancel."

Piper dutifully followed his cue. For having been together not more than fifteen minutes, she'd used her time rather judiciously. She returned the pad and pen to his desk, and then said, "I enjoyed catching up with you despite us not getting the script written. Why don't you shoot me a text with your available days and times? I'm sure we'll be able to work something out." She leaned over and embraced him in a friendly hug and then volunteered to show herself out.

As soon as Piper slammed her car door shut, she sent a text to Penelope asking her to call when she had a break. Piper had a hunch that the gallery, the missing library funds, and Brandt's murder were all connected. Penelope's insider status at the gallery would enable her to pinpoint any misdoings that could possibly link Reverend Black to the murder. Piper intended to flush out the responsible party even if all signs indicated that the holy man betrayed his comrade.

Most likely, Penelope would be tied up for the majority of the morning, so Piper decided to take a side trip to the library before heading to The Cardinal Shoppe. Her abruptness towards Mrs. B. the other day kept nagging at her conscience. Since she had some time to spare, Piper thought it best to check in on the sweet, older woman especially since Mrs. B. selflessly came to Piper's aid in her time of need.

An onslaught of patrons lingered near the front desk in anticipation of the re-shelving cart filled with new DVDs and music. The unsuspecting teenaged page with earbuds in her ears making her way out from behind the desk, barely noticed the caravan following closely behind. As soon as she abandoned the cart to shelve some materials, the pack charged, snatching up the highly desirable items before she returned. Piper stayed clear of the chaos by cutting through the children's area in order to get to Mrs. B.'s desk.

Goose bumps began popping up all over Piper's arms as she ambled down the long hallway. It didn't surprise her in the slightest as she was about to revisit the scene of the crime. When she peered around the corner, Piper spotted Mrs. B. seated at the desk with a pout on her face. The woman's dour expression didn't match her usual persona.

"Well, hello, Mrs. B.!" Piper shouted.

Mrs. B. looked up from whatever she was reading and said, "Piper! What a pleasant surprise!"

"I'm glad you think so. You didn't look too happy when I arrived."

Mrs. B. swiveled her chair around and then stood up. "Just dealing with some work nonsense, like usual. Come here. Let me give you a hug."

The two embraced and then congregated near her desk.

"What brings you by today?" Mrs. B. inquired. "Do you need to speak with Larry?"

"No, I came to see you. I thought I'd fill you in on my wedding plans. I was sort of pressed for time the other day," Piper said in an apologetic voice.

Mrs. B. clapped her hands together. "Oh, dear! Aren't you a breath of fresh air! Do tell!"

Piper followed through with her heartfelt intentions by sharing as much of the details as she possibly could without intruding on her work day. When the conversation began to lag, she switched topics to something a bit more pressing.

"I just ran into Desiree at the bagel shop and she said the Ball has sold out!"

Mrs. B. chimed in, "Good thing since the event is only four days away."

Piper responded, "That's wonderful news."

"Yes, indeed. Desiree mentioned to Larry that a late night surge of internet sales sent us over the top. As of this morning, there was a waiting list of approximately ten people. Who knew this event would be so popular!" Mrs. B. mused.

Piper took the compliment in stride knowing that she herself was the mastermind behind the event.

"I hate to cut our conversation short, but I have…"

"Oh, no problem. I'm headed into work anyway. I can only imagine how busy we are in anticipation of the big event. Lots to catch up on my end as well. I'm glad we had the chance to talk," Piper smiled.

"Me, too," she answered.

The two ladies said their goodbyes, and then Piper dashed over to the common area to pick up a new book to store under the counter at work. Not that she'd have time to read it today. A quick scan of the shelves revealed two hot bestsellers up for grabs. Pleased with her finds, she walked over to the check-out line and patiently waited her turn.

"I can help whoever's next," announced Mrs. Johnson.

Piper missed hearing the librarian call for the next patron as her attention was focused on her phone. The young gentleman behind her in line urged her on with a gentle tap on the shoulder. She thanked him for his kindness before taking her turn.

"Hi, Mrs. Johnson!" she said in an exceedingly cheerful manner in an effort to make up for her negligence. She placed her books on the counter and handed the librarian her worn library card.

"Holding up the line again, I see." The woman's derogatory remarks did little to dampen Piper's spirits.

"Exciting news about the ball, right? Sold out with only a week to spare. That's a relief! Will you be attending with Mr. Johnson?" Piper tried her best to engage the woman in light conversation.

The crotchety old lady looked Piper straight in the eyes and said, "No, he's dead."

Taken aback by the crassness of the remark, Piper spit out, "Well, good thing you didn't buy him a ticket then. No refunds."

Mrs. Johnson returned the two books to Piper along with a receipt. Even she couldn't help but be amused by the blonde's wit and charm. A tiny smile dared to escape from the librarian's lips as she watched Piper exit the building through the sliding glass doors.

The remainder of the afternoon flew by as Piper helped numerous customers narrow down their selections for the town's upcoming event. The constant stream of regular clients at The Cardinal Shoppe underscored the need for Piper to take notes as to who bought what dress to avoid duplications. Piper's foresight to supplement the inventory with one-of-a-kind wholesale gowns from well-known designers proved to be fortuitous. By three o'clock, the racks were nearly empty. Piper did her best to cope with frustrated customers, cranky children, and annoying husbands whose opinions interfered with her doing her job. More times than she cared to count, Piper had to explain to a customer that cleavage spilling over did not signify a good fit despite what hubby dearest had to say.

After the crowd thinned, Piper escaped to the back storeroom to rummage through the reserved stock held for special clientele only. She was in search of the perfect gown for Judge Halbreath. The woman's plus-size figure required a flattering silhouette to appropriately display her vivacious curves. Piper selected a vibrant green number adorned with a sprinkling of crystals that would accentuate her fellow board member's dark hair. The judge trusted Piper's professional opinion so much so that she agreed to purchase it sight unseen. Piper simply added the charge to the judge's tab and had the dress delivered to the courthouse along with a pair of low heels.

Liz thanked Piper for her superior customer service and rewarded her by sending her home early. Since she had clearly expended all her energy, Piper welcomed the opportunity to escape without having to fold the disorderly piles of clothes or straighten the racks.

Before she left the building, Piper grabbed two dresses tagged with her name from the storeroom. Naturally, as any fashionista would do, she had pre-selected the most exquisite gowns of the lot for Penelope and herself before stocking the floor. She couldn't wait to see Penelope's reaction when she unveiled the coveted picks.

Piper drove straight home to wait for her sister's arrival. The two had exchanged texts an hour ago to coordinate the details. Piper slipped into her cozy pajamas and pink fluffy robe and made herself a cup of decaf green tea. She plugged her phone into the wall charger and then curled up on the sofa with one of her recently checked out books. Her cat surfaced a few minutes later to investigate the contents of her mug. His disappointment over the lack of milk sent him on his way.

It didn't take long for Penelope to arrive, bounding into the house with two armfuls of packages. She insisted Piper stay seated as she made her way into the kitchen to prep their take-out dinner.

In the meantime, Piper removed the clutter from the coffee table and then set two coasters on each end. Ralph came out from hiding in hopes of snagging some table scraps from the gullible Penelope. The crafty feline played her like a fiddle when food was up for grabs.

Penelope entered the room with a tray brimming over with paper products, three cartons of Chinese food, a plateful of sushi, and two glasses of white wine. As she carefully placed it on the table, both Piper's and Ralph Lauren's mouths watered in anticipation of the scrumptious feast. Penelope handed her sister a white paper plate and proceeded to set a smaller version on the floor next to Ralph's tiny paws. A vociferous meow let the girls know the tomcat was more than ready to chow down.

The spur-of-the-moment party began with lots of good food and idle chatter from the sisters and feline alike. Hungry appetites were satiated as the sisters discussed the latest developments in the murder case. The wine continued to flow long after the food ran out. Later on, Piper took charge of the clean-up while Penelope relaxed on the couch with Ralphie who demanded her attention. After all the empty containers, plates, and used cutlery were discarded, Ralph ambled his way back to the kitchen, but not before licking his dirty paws clean.

"So, have you decided on a date for the ball?" Piper broached the sensitive subject. "I spoke with Rusty. We both are okay with you going with Jim, if that's what you'd like to do."

Penelope felt giddy. "Thanks for the approval, not that I needed it anyway," she said under her breath, "but I accepted an invitation to the ball from someone else. So, Jim will need to find himself another date if he still plans on attending."

"Really?" Piper was bewildered by her sister's news. "Mind sharing who the lucky gent is?" It was so unlike her sister to keep a secret.

Penelope's eyes shone brightly. "Reverend Black!"

Piper stared at her sister. "How did you manage to arrange that one?"

That was not the response her sister was expecting. "What do you mean 'arrange that one'?" Penelope demanded to know. "The most eligible bachelor in town called me up and asked me out on a date. And, I said yes! Is that so hard to believe?"

Piper tried a different approach. "You do realize that I have reason to believe Reverend Black was somehow involved with Brandt's murder, right?"

"Minor technicality, as far as I'm concerned. Until he's proven guilty, he's fair game. Lest you forget, you thought I was guilty, too. Look where that got you!" She was more than happy to point that out to her sister.

Piper insisted, "I never actually said that I thought you were guilty. I tried to prove your innocence, which I did, by the way."

Penelope begged to differ. "Not exactly, sis, but let's not rehash old news."

"Agreed." Piper kept quiet. The last thing she wanted to do was unnerve her little sister.

"So, are you going to show me the dress you bought for me, or do I have to guess what it looks like?" Penelope ruffled the garment bag that rested on the adjacent chair.

Piper swatted at her sister's hand. "Don't do that! You'll mess up the embellishments and then complain later on when I won't be able to fix the damage that you've done. Move over. Wait until you see what I snagged for you!"

Amid ooh's and ah's, Piper had the big reveal much to the delight of her little sis. First, she withdrew a gorgeous muted canary-colored gown for Penelope, laden with tiny pearl beading. Penelope squealed with delight at Piper's exquisite choice. Next, Piper removed a blush-colored, one-shoulder gown with a glistening overlay that screamed her name. Lastly, she showed her sister two pairs of sparkly, high-heeled shoes.

The next hour or so, the girls played dress up just like they did when younger. They would have continued into the wee hours of the night if it weren't for Penelope's need to get home. Unlike past jobs, she considered her work at the gallery of real significance. She even mentioned to Piper that she could see herself making career out of it. Before departing, Piper zipped her sister's gown back up in the garment bag and then returned the delicate shoes to the shoebox. Piper carried both outside and gently positioned them in the backseat of Penelope's car.

Piper tried once more to pry some info out of her sister as to how Reverend Black's invitation came to be...only to be shot right back down. Piper did manage to get Penelope to assure her that she'd keep both eyes wide open and report any suspicious behavior should any arise. Piper had no choice but to accept it for what it was for now. Her headstrong sister was notorious for making a point when she felt wronged. Piper sensed this was Penelope's way of getting back at her lack of transparency concerning Capt. Morgan's investigation. Only time would tell.

Back inside, Piper cleaned up the remainder of the mess and then headed upstairs to bed. Ralph followed closely behind. The old tomcat tired easily nowadays. Piper didn't know exactly how old he was seeing as she had rescued him from the shelter. Best guess, he was approaching his senior years. Nestled together in bed, Piper and her furry son nodded off to sleep. Their tranquil slumber didn't last long for Piper's churning stomach warranted a sudden trip to the bathroom. She made a mental note to call the doctor in the morning about her lingering sinus infection. The antibiotics didn't seem to agree so much with her sensitive stomach.

When Piper crawled back into bed, she tried to lull herself back to sleep by meditating. Her attempt at creating a peaceful Zen didn't last for long. The incessant binging from her cell phone broke the silence. Piper leaned over and grabbed it from the bedside table. Sure enough, she had a stream of text messages from queen bee Carolyn asking to meet at the ball venue early in the morning to review the floor plan. Why the woman felt the need to reach out at one in the morning was beyond comprehensible. Piper sent off a brief text in return, confirming the time and place and then switched her phone to silent. Soon after, the exhaustion from the day finally caught up with her. She rolled over to her left side and reached out to the empty space next to her. Longing for Rusty's soft touch, she closed her eyes and slowly drifted off to sleep.

Chapter 15
Comments from the Public

"This area should be designated for the VIP bar," Carolyn pointed through the windows to a picturesque outdoor space. "The fountain will make a stunning backdrop for photos. Speaking of which, I acted upon your recommendation and hired your so-called family friend. He better be as good as you say he is or you'll be hearing from me." Another unexpected rain shower prevented access to the outside.

"Remind me again exactly what perks come with the VIP status?" Piper shuffled through the numerous papers Carolyn had handed to her upon their arrival.

Carolyn recited verbatim the cushy details. "Early access to the event. Prime parking spot at the venue. One complimentary raffle ticket for the diamond and ruby ring."

"And, what is the added cost for these benefits?"

"An extra fifty dollars per ticket. My ingenious idea generated more than twenty-five hundred extra. We cut it off at fifty people," Carolyn informed her. "Of course, any company that sponsored the event also received VIP access. So, all told, there will be approximately seventy-five people in this area."

"Rusty and I will definitely take advantage of the view and snap a bunch of selfies. Ooh! I'll have to remember to bring my selfie stick." Piper raised her eyebrows.

Carolyn replied, "Why does that not surprise me?"

"Our wedding will be here before you know it. We are tying the knot December twenty-eighth. Mark your calendar." Piper beamed with joy.

"Really? A December wedding? How festive!" Carolyn said in reply.

"Seriously though, I'm glad you finally came to your senses at the last minute and listened to January. Switching to this location situated on the fringe of the county was totally worth it. With all the renovations going on at the club, it just makes perfect sense to have it here at this glorious estate." Piper eyed the sweeping staircase in the foyer. "Wow! Take a look at that antique grandfather clock perched at the top of the stairs! It's absolutely gorgeous. The chiming of the bells will help us keep track of the minutes during the event."

Less than a week earlier, a violent rainstorm rolled through Woodlawn causing a hundred-year-old tree to uproot. It crashed through the ceiling of the main dining room at the club causing considerable damage to the facility. January pulled some strings by convincing the owners of a magnificent family estate to allow the function to be moved there for a nominal fee. Luckily, the club agreed to refund the full deposit due to the freak act of nature. The library ball would be able to proceed as planned without any financial repercussions.

"Let's move on and review the appetizer and serving stations since we don't have room for a sit down dinner. It's going to be a little tricky blending those in with the elaborate décor of the house. We have permission to remove some furniture. Why don't we start at the entrance and make our way through the house as if we were party guests." Carolyn's suggestion was more of a directive rather than an off-the-cuff remark. Side by side, the two women worked efficiently, pinpointing the troublesome areas like a couple of loose bannisters requiring attention and some squeaky floorboards. They also compiled a short list of furniture in need of temporary storage. By the time they were through, the layout for the affair had been agreed upon without any conflicting issues holding them back.

"Thank you, Piper, for your valuable input and assistance. Truth be told, I'm surprised everything went so smoothly, considering we don't always see eye to eye." Carolyn stuffed her notes into her carryall. "Oh, and I love my dress for the ball. I hate to admit that I should have listened to you in the first place. My husband agreed my first choice made me look rather matronly."

Piper jingled the car keys in her hand. "You're welcome on all counts. Glad I could be of help. Do you have a few minutes to talk? I have something I've been meaning to ask you."

Carolyn checked her watch. "I suppose so. My mani/pedi appointment isn't until after lunch. Let me guess. You want me to be in your wedding party. I figured it was just a matter of time before you popped the question. Piper, dear, you unashamedly hinted at it when you mentioned the wedding date earlier. I'd have to be deaf, dumb, and blind not to realize what you were implying."

Flustered by the inane comments spewing from her frenemy's lips, Piper spluttered, "Um…"

Carolyn continued, "Of course, darling, you'd want your dearest Woodlawn friend to witness your marital union front and center. The answer is yes, on one condition."

"And, wh…what would that be?" Piper dared to ask.

"I refuse to wear pink." Carolyn threw up her hands in protest.

"Oh, no!" Piper exclaimed in her best thespian voice possible. "That's what I selected!" Piper's rapid heartbeat slowly returned to a normal rhythm. Thank goodness for Carolyn's aversion to Piper's signature color.

"That color just doesn't suit my skin tone. Not one hue of pink flatters my pale complexion. Believe you me. I've tried. Listen, I'm truly honored, Piper, that you asked me to partake in your special day, but I must decline. Will you ever be able to forgive me?" She stepped forward and took hold of Piper's hands.

Piper hung her head low for full dramatic effect and then whispered, "Of course."

"Thank you, darling." Carolyn flashed her pageant girl smile.

Piper deemed it wise to carry on, seeing as the two had struck a harmonious chord that day. "How well do you know Nancy Flagstone?"

Carolyn paused for a moment and then said, "We've played in the same bridge group every Thursday afternoon at the club off and on for the last five years or so. Why do you ask?"

Piper chose her words carefully. "It must have been comforting for her to have you as a dear confidante when she and Larry made the choice to subconsciously uncouple."

"What? That doesn't even make sense, Piper. Nah, I'd say it was more along the lines of an epic dissolution or maybe even a mass destruction. Larry never saw it coming. Poor, pathetic soul. The man trembles to this day if her name is even mentioned. By the way, Larry has no clue that she and I are casual acquaintances, so please refrain from mentioning our connection. You know me well enough. I make it a point to stay clear of any drama. As far as I'm concerned, my hands are clean." Carolyn pretended to wipe her hands as if trying to convince herself that her comment was indeed true.

"I don't mean to pry, but did they have any financial troubles while married?" Piper watched Carolyn formulate an answer.

"From what I understand, Nancy comes from money. So when the divorce was finalized, Larry was left with a meager allowance, if you will," Carolyn explained.

"Interesting," Piper commented.

"Why do you ask?" Carolyn shifted her purse from one shoulder to the other.

"I shared with you my concern over the missing Friends' money, and all evidence points to Nancy as the voice of authority on the subject. Yet, pinning this woman down for a discussion on the topic appears to be a Herculean task. Before I engage in what could be confrontational, I'd like to do my homework concerning Nancy's background, especially her money sense," Piper reasoned.

"Then why are you wasting your time speaking with me? Go talk with Chuck. He and Nancy are childhood friends. If anyone has the scoop on Nancy, believe you me it would be Chuck Loudon. Of course, please..."

Piper finished her sentence, "don't tell him I sent you."

"Exactly! See, you're catching on, Piper." Carolyn complimented her and then left for the nail salon.

It took a mere five minutes for Piper to zoom over to Chuck's hardware shop on Main Street. She pulled into the first available parking space and wasted no time hightailing it into the store. The front window of the store was papered with sale signs. Once inside, Piper was met by the voice of an unsatisfied customer ranting over the unfavorable shade of paint she had purchased. The teenaged sales clerk hemmed and hawed while trying to come up with an amenable solution. Just when it appeared the situation was about to spin out of control, Chuck emerged from the rear of the store. Within the span of ten minutes, the customer received a full refund plus a complimentary gallon of neutral paint to cover her 'horrendous mistake.'

Chuck didn't notice Piper milling about in the power tool section of the expansive store. As he made his way back to his office, he nearly knocked her over.

"Piper!" He grabbed her wrist to prevent his colleague from tumbling over. "I didn't see you standing there. You okay?"

Piper regained her composure. "Good save!" she joked.

"Is there something in particular I can help you find?" Chuck rested his lumberjack-sized arm on a nearby display.

"I'm in search of a new power tool for Rusty. Sort of like a premarital gift." Her attempt at camouflaging her purported agenda was weak at best.

"Then you have come to the right place. Let me show you our top sellers," he said.

Piper exhaled a sigh of relief.

Chuck did his best to schmooze Piper by showing her the most expensive items in his inventory with the hopes of scoring a cha-ching of a big sale. He even offered a generous friend discount to sweeten the deal. Just when Piper couldn't bear listening to another one of his sales pitches, she interjected, "I bumped into an old friend of yours the other day...Nancy Firestone...I mean Flagstone. Nancy Flagstone. She sends her greetings."

Her innocuous comment caught Chuck completely off-guard. Rather than reply with a typical generic response such as 'tell her hello' or 'she's a nice lady,' he chose to remain silent. An odd response from a man who supposedly knew this woman all his life. Piper felt the need to delve a little deeper, seeing as Chuck wouldn't budge an inch.

"I understand the two of you go way back. Grade school, I heard." Piper pretended to browse the merchandise while waiting for him to say something.

"Yeah, we know each other. I know almost everybody in this town one way or another. I've lived here all my life," Chuck stated matter-of-factly.

Piper edged closer to the leaf blower. "You know, I had no idea that the Nancy from the Friends group that we've been talking about and Larry's ex-wife were one and the same until recently when we met. Small world."

Chuck just nodded his head to acknowledge what she'd said.

In a last ditch effort to get him talking, Piper pushed a little further, "It's such a shame what happened between Nancy and Larry."

All of sudden Chuck blurted out, "Yes, Piper. I slept with her! There! I said it. What you obviously heard is true. It was a stupid mistake, but I wasn't the first and I won't be the last. That conniving woman seduced me! She knew exactly what she was doing. I was three sheets to the wind at the firemen's fundraiser and she zeroed in. Took full advantage of my inebriated state. And then, to come clean to Larry in the middle of the grocery store on a Sunday morning after church, for heaven's sake! She couldn't have waited until she got home. The whole town was practically listening to her confess in the middle of the canned fruit aisle. All I have to say is thank goodness my wife forgave me."

Piper stood there with her mouth hanging wide-open. Not the most lady-like pose, but appropriately merited for what she'd just heard. Grappling for something inoffensive to say in response, she fiddled with her purse strap as an excuse for not speaking.

"So is that the real reason why you stopped by my store today, Piper? To hear the story straight from the source?" The veins on his forehead bulged with aggression.

"Oh, no! Not at all, Chuck. To be honest, I had no idea the two of you, um, tangoed so to speak," Piper confessed. "I have reason to believe that Nancy may be in cahoots with someone concerning the disappearance of funds. And, I know this may sound far-fetched, but I think she also may be linked to Brandt's murder."

"Sweet, mother, Mary. Why didn't you say that in the first place?" Chuck demanded.

"And miss out on that tantalizing scoop, heck no!" Piper admitted.

Rather than scold Piper for her deception, Chuck ushered her into his back office to discuss Nancy's theoretical misdoings. He took preventative steps to ward off the possibility of being overhead by a nosy customer by closing the office door. The two conferred for over thirty minutes, comparing mental notes and snippets of gossip in a spirited conversation. The co-conspirators aimed to pin both crimes on Nancy should their evidence prove her guilt. Sometime in the middle of their discussion, a young salesclerk barged into the office in search of a roll of paper for the register only to be sent away by the sound of Chuck's vociferous scolding. Imagine the employee's surprise at finding his boss sequestered in the back office with a hot blonde like Piper. The fella winked at Chuck on his way out the door as if signaling some secret bro-code. The effort was lost on Chuck, seeing as he was fully engrossed in the matter at hand.

Piper would have stayed longer if it wasn't for a surprise visit by Chuck's beloved wife. Her arrival warranted a rapid-fire explanation by Chuck for the need of such a clandestine rendezvous. Piper did her best to reassure the feisty, petite woman that her cuddly bear only had eyes for his beautiful wife.

On her way out of the office, Piper spotted a cache of paintings hidden behind an open door leading down to the cellar. From her viewpoint, she could spy a picturesque landscape scene with a babbling brook in the foreground. She hoped to get a better look but Chuck was trailing close behind with his suspicious wife. Piper preferred not to create more havoc so she made up a plausible excuse to explain her hasty retreat.

By then, it was approaching lunchtime and Piper's grumbling tummy bellowed to be fed. The diner's close proximity prompted her to pay it a visit. Dining alone did not excite her; however, her desire for a turkey club sandwich and sweet tea prevailed. Once inside the joint, she spotted Judge Halbreath dining at the counter alone with her nose pressed between the pages of the daily newspaper. The vacant chair beside her beckoned for Piper's booty to fill it.

"Is this seat taken?" Piper asked.

Judge Halbreath folded the newspaper into quarters and then laid it on the counter for later. "Well, hello, Piper! Take a seat, my esteemed colleague. I've been meaning to call you anyway. We have some things to discuss, in private."

Choosing to stop by the diner was turning out to be quite fortuitous for Piper. Satisfying her hunger while digesting some prime scoop from the town's most credible source couldn't be better. Piper hadn't been seated more than fifteen seconds when Suzy, the perky waitress with bedroom eyes for Jay, presented her with a chilled sweet tea.

"Here you go, sugar. Would you like the usual turkey club and fries with a side of honey mustard?" Her bright smile radiated cheerfulness.

Piper replied, "Yes, please!"

"You got it, honey." Suzy headed towards the kitchen.

Judge Halbreath folded the newspaper into quarters and then laid it on the counter until later. "With the town abuzz about the impending ball, it's left no time for us to discuss the relevant issues affecting the library. As treasurer, you must weigh heavily the pros and cons of the various options for retirement benefits and healthcare plans for the employees and then present your recommendations to the executive committee in a swift manner. We've been putting it off due to Brandt's sudden pronouncement to depart from the board."

Piper thought Judge Halbreath's interpretation of Brandt's death rather peculiar. The man didn't choose to depart by his own free will.

"Has Chuck shared the information with you?" she inquired.

"As a matter of fact, he did send me an email with a slew of attachments, but I haven't had time to sort through them yet," Piper admitted.

Suzy delivered Piper's lunch complete with a bonus side of coleslaw. "The chef made it fresh this morning. Figured you'd want some." She scooted away before Piper had a chance to properly thank the waitress for her small act of kindness.

"Do you and Chuck have a strong preference for any of the plans?" Piper figured it would be best to pick the woman's brains before selecting an unpopular choice.

Judge Halbreath took a sip of coffee.

"With your prior experience in dealing with these issues, I'd greatly appreciate your input." Piper dipped one quarter of the club sandwich into the honey mustard and then took a generous bite.

"That, doll, is totally up to you. Sift through each one and keep a tally of the advantages and disadvantages. Once you feel confident with your selection, write up your recommendation. If nothing else, this tedious exercise will prove useful one day when you become a small business owner. Think of it as a learning tool of sorts." Judge Halbreath signaled for Suzy to bring over the check.

"Small business owner? I never said I was going to open my own store," Piper clarified.

Judge Halbreath gathered her belongings, "You're too ambitious not to, my dear. Your boss Liz will be retiring in the near future. I've heard the rumor circulating among my social circle, so it must be true."

Piper snickered at the irony of that statement.

"Being a salesclerk is not your future. No, Piper, greater things are in store for you...just ask Shep. Playing second fiddle is never any fun. The ultimate victory comes at the very moment when you, my dear, are the one calling all the shots. Think about it. Being denied what some believe rightfully belongs to them sometimes causes unstable individuals to do dangerous things."

The wise, mature judge kissed her protégé on both cheeks and then left Piper alone to ponder what she'd just said.

Piper wasn't exactly sure why, but she had a distinct feeling that amid Judge Halbreath's professional advice was hidden a pivotal clue to Brandt's murder case. Trying to decipher what the woman meant would prove to be the bigger challenge.

Piper planned to nibble on her lunch a bit longer, but the graveness of it all caused her interest to wane. Even her fickle stomach balked at the idea. When she summoned Suzy, Piper discovered the judge had already covered the check. Piper left a generous tip and then changed course. A quick side trip to Jay's office to get his take on the situation was in order. Even though she'd promised to attend to the library's pressing business, she decided to skip it for the time being. She didn't have the patience for sorting through copious documents nor for constructing charts to keep track of her findings. For now, her primary concern was Brandt's murder case.

Even though a wealth of evidence pointed to Nancy as the culpable party, Piper was beginning to have serious doubts. In the back of her mind, she couldn't help but shake the feeling that she had overlooked someone more obvious, but who? Her grandiose plan to solicit Jay never came to fruition as she received a frantic phone call from Desiree concerning another issue with the Booklovers' Ball. At first, Piper planned on sending the call over to voicemail. Dealing with Desiree would require Piper's full attention, a scarce commodity at best. But, at the last second she changed her mind and answered the call. Call it a hunch, but something told her that Desiree held the key to Brandt's murder case. The only way to unlock the proverbial door involved Piper earning the conniving ingénue's trust.

"No, it's no imposition at all." Piper's exaggerated sugary drawl was intended to catch flies. "Sure, I'll be right over."

Chapter 16
Adjournment of Public Meeting

Piper arrived at the library armed with her trusty purse, a pad of paper, and a pencil she found stashed in the driver's side door compartment. She waved hello to Mrs. Johnson who sat primly at the information desk waiting to pounce on her next victim. Piper surveyed the area in search of Desiree who had earlier claimed to be circulating in the common area. No sign of her so far. While Piper was rounding the corner, she accidentally slammed into Larry who was carrying a stack of files. As she watched oodles of paper flutter up into the air and then descend onto the carpeted floor, all she could think of was the saying…let it rain. In true Larry fashion, he summoned Mrs. B. on the intercom at the help desk to come collect the scattered mess. Piper scolded the fearless leader for being a lazy oaf and proceeded to get down on her hands and knees to contribute her fair share.

It came as no surprise that Mrs. B. disapproved of his ridiculous behavior as well, for she reluctantly picked up some file folders and placed them on a nearby study carrel. Her working at a snail's pace frustrated Larry to no end causing him to join in despite himself. The threesome was able to get everything picked up in no time.

"What brings you by the library?" Larry shuffled some papers together to straighten the pile.

Piper replied, "I'm here to see Desiree."

Unnerved by her answer, Larry stammered, "Wh…why?"

At that moment, a strikingly beautiful woman approached the group. Having never met Nancy in person, Piper couldn't say with certainty that this woman was she. But by the way Larry's demeanor instantly changed from displaying his puffed up chest to now having his shoulders hunched over, Piper felt confident she was the one.

"Well, look who it is. Larry, dear. Funny I should run into you here. Desiree said you'd be out of the building on business. Are you on your way out the door? Don't let little ol' me stop you from your official duties." She waved her arm as if showing him to the door. Nancy gave him an obvious once over as if intentionally trying to intimidate him. Needless to say, Larry's disheveled appearance did little to boost his already low self-confidence.

"Um, ummm…" Larry couldn't spit the words out.

Piper stepped right in. "Hello." She extended her hand in greeting. "You must be Nancy Flagstone. So nice to finally meet you! My future father-in-law speaks so highly of you. My name is Piper O'Donnell. I'm the newly-appointed treasurer for the board of trustees."

Nancy obliged by shaking Piper's hand and then retreated a few steps back. "And, whom may I ask is your future father-in-law?"

Piper paused for full effect. "Capt. Morgan." Sensing the woman's uncomfortable vibe, Piper showed her who was boss by inching closer, "I understand we have lots of catching up to do." Piper held Nancy's hand in her own a little bit longer than customary…just because. The much-anticipated showdown had finally begun.

In an effort to extricate himself from the conversation, Larry interjected, "I'll just leave you two to sort things out." He glanced at his wrist and then said, "Oh, no! I'm late for a meeting."

"How can you tell? You have no watch on your wrist, bozo. What are you using to tell time these days? Your freckles?" Nancy's condescending tone did not go unnoticed by all gathered.

Mrs. B. looped her arm around Larry's. "I beg your pardon. I'm the one who informed him of such."

Still befuddled by Nancy's pointed barbs, Larry turned and faced Mrs. B. "You did?"

Mrs. B. stared him right back in the eyes. "I most certainly did."

Just then, Piper noticed Desiree come into view. As soon as Desiree locked eyes with Piper, she quickened her pace to join the huddle. "Hello! I see everyone is present." She folded her hands together. "Shall we convene to Larry's office now? We have lots of ground to cover in a short amount of time."

The entourage cautiously proceeded to the rear of the building. Like a herd of sheep, Desiree gently prodded them along, being careful not to let them wander from her sight. Once inside the office, she pointed each one to the assigned chair that contained a placard with the person's name taped to the back. Without waiting for instruction, Larry assumed his position at the helm. Mrs. B. flipped open her steno book in preparation for taking copious notes. All the while, Piper reviewed the financial sheets left on her seat for her perusal.

"Thank you all for coming together for this vital meeting," Desiree began. "As you are fully aware, the ball is just days away. In order to facilitate an undertaking of this magnitude, all entities of the library system—the Friends, board of trustees, and the administration—must cooperate in order to make it a huge success. At this juncture, it has come to Larry's attention that the presumed missing funds have been located." Desiree shot Larry a deliberate look.

"They have?" Larry chimed.

Desiree's obvious disappointment of her boss's ignorance caused her to say, "Yes, Larry. They have. Remember?" She shook her head in agreement.

Mrs. B. and Piper looked at each other in an attempt to figure out what was going on. Sadly, neither was able to provide a clue.

"So now that our coffers are full, we can put to rest this unsavory rumor." Desiree nervously cracked a smile.

Piper wouldn't allow Desiree the pleasure of getting off so easily. "Would you please clarify to all present exactly how these missing funds came to be found?"

Nancy answered Piper's question. "I think what Desiree is trying to say is that the funds were never missing. After a thorough examination, I was able to verify that the moneys were credited to the capital fund rather than to the foundation as originally planned. With the recent improvements to the branch, the account had significantly fluctuated, signaling to us a big red flag. When I brought it to Larry's attention, he was able to rectify the situation. Nothing to worry about, Piper. It's all there."

Once again, Larry questioned, "It is?"

Nancy glowered at him. "Yes, Larry. Every last cent."

Piper's reluctance to counter with another query was interpreted as an acceptance of the story told. Nothing could be farther from the truth. If Piper had to wager a guess, she'd put her money on Nancy. Something didn't add up, but now wasn't the time to question it.

"Well then, I guess we're finished here." Piper abruptly stood up.

Desiree seemed rather relieved that Piper didn't balk at the explanation. "Um, thanks, Piper for stopping by on such short notice."

"You may want to send out an email to the board explaining what we just discussed. I'm sure they'll be very interested in hearing the good news," Piper recommended.

Desiree promised she'd take care of it within the hour.

"Nancy," Piper said. "As you can imagine, my schedule is booked solid for the next couple of days. Perhaps we'll be able to chat at the ball. I'm looking forward to working closely with you." Piper's emphasis on the word *closely* did not sit well with Larry for he cringed at its mention.

Nancy forced a smile, but said not a word. Her silence spoke volumes to all present.

The awkward exchange between the two women prompted Larry to take action. "Piper, why don't I escort you to your car?" He juxtaposed himself at her side. "We need to discuss the healthcare plans and retirement benefits for the library staff."

Before leaving the room, Mrs. B. mentioned something to Larry *sotto voce* that caused him to scoff. The glum expression on her face betrayed the old woman's feelings. She did not appreciate his blatant disregard for what she had to say.

Piper and Larry exited the building using one of the side doors. Once outside, Piper let him have it. "What did you say that upset Mrs. B.?"

"Nothing that concerns you," he replied rather haughtily.

Piper clicked the remote control on her key ring to unlock her vehicle. "If I didn't know any better, I'd say you were hiding something. Speaking of which, I'd have appreciated a heads-up concerning your battle-axe ex-wife. What the heck were you thinking marrying her?"

Larry sighed, "I agree. Not my best decision."

"I'd say," Piper commented. "So what did you want to talk about? I don't have much time to waste. Believe it or not, I do have somewhere else to be." She glanced at her pink watch.

"Oh," Larry said. "Yes, we need to come to a decision regarding all the benefits. Going forward, I don't think the library can sustain funding these plans at the same rate. There needs to be a major reduction in benefit costs across the board. Granted, this proposal will not be well-received by the employees, especially those nearing retirement, but it's financially necessary to ensure our viability."

"And, how did Brandt lean towards this issue? Was he for or against it?" Piper asked.

Larry didn't miss a beat. "He favored it despite the grumblings of those closest to him."

"I have a strong feeling the board was split down the middle on this motion. Am I right?" she questioned.

Larry hedged his bets. "Let's just say their views tended to be quite divergent. The board needs a voice of reason to steer them in the right direction. I was kinda hoping that would be you." He pointed his finger straight at her.

"So basically what you're saying is that I need to infiltrate the opposing side with my wit, charm, and beauty so that I can convince them to vote for these drastic cuts, right?" Piper folded her arms across her chest. "That is, if I think this proposed option best suits the future of the library as a whole."

"Keep talking," Larry urged her on.

"That's a lot of responsibility you're throwing at me, Mr. Library Director. Technically, this is my first rodeo, cowboy." Piper grabbed a lock of her blonde hair and twisted it around her finger. "I'm going to have to take some time and diligently review the documents. I see no other way. How about if I get back to you by maybe Friday of next week? Would that work?"

Larry rocked back and forth on his toes contemplating his answer. "Um, how about by Monday?"

"The week after next? Yes, that's probably even a better suggestion," Piper agreed.

Larry replied, "No, Piper. I mean this coming Monday at our regularly scheduled board meeting."

"Are you for real? How do you expect me to sift through the mountain of paperwork in two days? The ball is Tuesday night! I have so much to do this weekend to get ready. I realize you must think I get up every morning looking as radiant as I do now, but that's not true. It takes more than just lotions and potions to get me looking this fabulous," Piper insisted.

Larry tried a different approach. "If it were Carolyn in this position, yes, I couldn't agree more. There's no way she could handle all the pressure without cracking. But, you! You, Piper, are not the typical woman. You're strong!"

"Yes!" Piper punched her fist up in the air.

"Talented!" he sang out.

"Yes!" she rejoiced while waving her hands above her head.

"And..."

"Not stupid!" she exclaimed.

His attempt to flatter her fell flat.

"C'mon, Larry. I know what you're trying to do and it won't work."

Larry had no choice but to play hardball. "Your options are limited. We're meeting on Monday and this item will be on the agenda. How you spend your weekend is your business. When we convene, I'll expect you to put forward a recommendation. Then, a fellow board member will present a motion and a vote will be taken. If I were you, I'd spend tonight and tomorrow pouring over the documents. From my experience, its best to come fully armed with information lest you leave looking like a fool. If you need anything, you know how to reach me. I hope you make the right decision for yourself as well as the library."

And with that, Larry shuffled back into the building.

Frustrated by the stringent parameters imposed upon her, Piper sped off in search of a sympathetic ear. She bet the one person who would gladly commiserate with her would most likely be half-asleep at his desk. When she entered the office, there he was half comatose with drool dripping from the corner of his mouth. The sight warmed her heart to the fullest. She pushed his feet off the edge of the desk causing him to snap to attention.

"I was researching the …." he jabbered.

"Hush. It's only me," Piper assured him. "You're lucky your dad didn't find you. I need your help."

Jay rubbed his eyes with his fists.

"Am I keeping you awake?" she whined.

"Kind of," he admitted while slinking down in his chair.

Piper joined him by propping her feet up on the trash can. "Any news on the murder case?"

Jay grabbed hold of the lapels on his jacket. "Nah, but I did get myself a date for the ball."

Piper righted herself up. "You stud muffin. Who's the lucky girl?"

"Suzy from the diner," he announced. "She asked if I wanted to double-date with Penelope and Reverend Black. I said sure! Why not?"

"Really? That's news to me. It would have been nice for my sister to have filled me in on that little detail, but I guess that's too much to ask." Piper fumed.

"Sorry, Piper. It only happened yesterday," he disclosed.

"Wait, wait, wait!" she shouted. "That's perfect. Now you can be my spy. Jay, you need to get the preacher crazy drunk and pump him for details. Think you can do it?"

Jay hopped to his feet. "It would be my pleasure!"

"I think I'm on the cusp of figuring out who killed Brandt, my friend," she informed him.

Jay placed his hand on her shoulder. "Want to share your newsworthy idea with yours truly?"

All of a sudden, Piper felt her insides gurgling.

"Hungry?" Jay asked her.

"Actually, no," she said. "My stomach is upset. I think I better head home."

Jay shook his head. "Lame excuse, Piper O'Donnell, for not wanting to fill me in. I thought we were in this together. You're copping out on me."

Piper stumbled while getting up. "Seriously, Jay. I've been having stomach issues. I swear those antibiotics did me in. No joke." She rubbed her tummy. "Before I take off, I will say that I'm more than convinced that Nancy shoved that bookcase over and killed Brandt. I just can't for the life of me figure out why."

"Maybe he was on to her about the missing funds," he suggested.

"Oh, I forgot to tell you. Long story, but I was at a meeting at the library before I stopped by here and Desiree announced that the funds have been recovered, so to speak. Supposedly, the moneys were credited to the wrong account. Likely story, if you ask me. I didn't voice my doubts. Instead, I made believe that I was okay with it. We need to get our hands on Nancy's financial records. Think you could ask your sweet cousin to look into it? I know she's the guilty one. She has to be," Piper ranted.

"You go home and climb into bed. You need to be on your A game for the ball. I'll take care of the snooping. If I find anything out, I'll be in touch." He kissed the top of her head. "Trust me. You look beat."

Piper followed her friend's suggestion and hurried home. It didn't take long before she was fast asleep on the living room sofa with Ralphie neatly curled in the crook of her legs.

Nightfall approached while the two peacefully slumbered. If it wasn't for Rusty fiddling with the pots and pans in the cupboard, the two would have slept right through until morning.

"Sorry, babe. I didn't mean to wake you. I thought I'd reheat the soup Helen sent over for dinner. Looks like you could use some nourishment. I couldn't find the lid for the sauce pan." Rusty squeezed his bottom on the edge of the cushion. He whispered naughty thoughts into her ear as he gently massaged her back.

Piper swatted at him. "That's the last thing I need to be doing!"

He laughed.

"Any news from Capt. Morgan?" Piper couldn't let the murder case rest.

Rusty crouched down to the floor and pulled her right on top of him. "I'll only tell if you kiss me three times."

Piper pecked him three times on alternate cheeks similar to a sexy French woman. "I don't want to get you sick," she explained.

"Fair enough," he conceded. "Capt. Morgan is close to nabbing the killer. I overheard him on a conference call that he plans on setting a trap at the ball."

"No kidding?" Excitement ran through Piper's veins. "Any mentioning of names?"

Rusty sat upright and eased her onto his lap. "No, but he kept using the pronoun 'she'."

Piper beat his chest with her fists. "I'm right! It's Nancy."

"Whoa, whoa, whoa there, Barbie doll," he cautiously grabbed her wrists. "It's not like Capt. Morgan smacked an emblem on her back saying murderer. You're assuming he's speaking of Nancy. We don't know that for sure. You're going to have to keep a lid on this, babe, or else you're going to spoil the plan."

Piper weaseled her way out of his clutches. "No worries!" she assured him. She made her way into the kitchen. "I get to spend the next twenty-four hours or so immersed in library mumbo-jumbo. I won't have time to trouble myself with the murder details. C'mon. Where's that soup you were talking about? My appetite has returned with a vengeance."

As the engaged couple snuggled in front of the hearth, satiating their hunger with Helen's scrumptious homemade soup, across town Brandt's murderer busied the night away choreographing the final steps of what potentially could be Piper's fatal finale at the Booklovers' Ball.

Chapter 17
Executive Session

Sunday came and went as Piper executed her due
diligence concerning the proposed healthcare and
retirement plans. With the help of pie charts and graphs,
she identified the pros and cons of each, taking into
account the financial gains for the library as well as the
number of employees potentially impacted by her
recommendation. The piecemeal approach took more
time than she had anticipated. The day flew by as she
sequestered herself inside her home without once
checking her texts or emails. If she was going to take
the time to do this then she needed to do it right. Once
Piper had finished her comprehensive analysis, she felt
more confident with her decision. If nothing else, she
had a better understanding of the situation and what
was truly at stake.

When Monday rolled around, Piper started off the
day at The Cardinal Shoppe, checking in with her
preferred clients about their purchases for tomorrow
night's ball. She needed a break from all the stress
concerning the impending board meeting. Instead, she
was in her element pairing dresses with glistening
baubles and glitzy shoes. As usual, some last minute
lulu belles came in expecting to find a ball gown in
their size and favorite color only to be gravely
disappointed. By closing time, Piper's feet ached from
waiting on customers all day. She had just enough time
to change into a suit and grab a cup of coffee before
heading over to the library for the board meeting.

Behind the wheel, random thoughts popped into Piper's head as she meandered along the way. Always the optimist, she firmly believed her fellow board members would be in agreement once she presented her findings. She was well prepared to field some difficult questions from Chuck and maybe Judge Halbreath, but as Larry explained to her, the well-being of the library was at stake. Surely, they would be able to see the bigger picture. Since it was a public meeting, Piper wondered if any inquiring citizens would be in attendance. Most nights, the seats were filled with employees charged with the task of making a special presentation to the board. It was a true rarity to have a comment from the public.

As Piper entered the building, the sight of Mrs. Johnson at her designated spot gave Piper a sense of comfort. All was well at the library that night. The building had its fair share of patrons milling about in search of their next literary adventure. Piper didn't dawdle for she needed a few extra minutes to scribble some notes on the infamous white board. She wanted to be fully prepared before she launched into her spiel.

Inside the board room, most of her colleagues were already present. Their prompt attendance threw Piper off balance since she'd hoped to have a few extra minutes alone in the room to prepare. She chided herself for not leaving the store earlier. The last thing she needed to do was botch this presentation in front of her peers.

Larry and Chuck compared notes as to which baseball team would make it to the World Series. Piper secretly hoped their nonsensical exchange would endure a bit longer. Mrs. B. busied herself with her assigned duties of setting up the sound system and passing out the board packets. Carolyn, January, and the judge were engaged in an animated discussion about their attire for the Booklovers' Ball. With any luck, they wouldn't notice the clock quickly approaching the starting time. Surprisingly, the reverend and Desiree were nowhere to be found. Piper didn't have time to waste theorizing as to their whereabouts.

After some brief hellos, Piper stashed her purse under the table at her assigned seat. She then proceeded to the front of the room in search of the white board. Attired in her favorite pink suit, she had all the confidence she needed in order to take charge of the situation. At least that was what she was telling herself over and over in her head. She scribbled some acronyms with financial figures alongside some important dates. She also made two columns and headed them *pros* and *cons*. Taking a step back, she evaluated what she'd written for a moment. Satisfied with the results, she returned to her seat.

At two minutes prior to the start of the meeting, Reverend Black and Desiree waltzed through the doorway and quickly took their seats without acknowledging anyone in the room. Larry tried to catch Desiree's eyes but to no avail. She deliberately averted his stare in favor of the stack of papers neatly piled in front of her. As for Judge Halbreath, she raised an eyebrow at Piper who discreetly shrugged her shoulders in response. Whatever those two were up to, the others would have to wait patiently to see.

Judge Halbreath wasted no time in starting the meeting. She whipped through the preliminary parts of the agenda in an effort to save time for the important matters. It was no secret the majority of the evening would be spent hashing out the details of the retirement benefits and healthcare plans. Halfway through the meeting, a small group of familiar faces led by Mrs. Johnson crowded into the board room. One by one, they filled the vacant seats lining the back wall. Piper clenched her teeth worrying about the potential fallout from her forthcoming recommendations to the board by those gathered in the room. In an effort to boost her self-confidence, Piper shifted around in her chair as to avoid making eye contact with anyone in the rear.

When the time finally arrived for the action items, Judge Halbreath addressed the personnel changes first. She started with the resignations and new hires. Not much movement among the ranks. Next, a couple of senior librarians had submitted their notices for retirement effective at the end of the month. Larry publically acknowledged them for their twenty-plus years of service to the library. He also announced that Mrs. B. would be coordinating the festivities to properly honor the individuals. Further details would be shared in the coming weeks. As a sidebar, he joked with Mrs. B. for not turning in her resignation as well. The spry old woman made a snarky remark that caused a ripple of laughter to break out. The judge reprimanded the group, asking them to focus solely on the business at hand.

"Next item on the agenda pertains to the reevaluation of the retirement benefits and heath care options for our librarians and staff. As you may recall, we discussed these options at length under Brandt's leadership, but we were unable to come to an agreement. We have now reached a crucial point where a decision must come forth from this governing body. For the good of the library, Piper accepted the daunting task of evaluating each plan and is now ready to make a solid recommendation to the board. It is my hope that we'll be able to finalize our decision this evening. So, without further ado, Piper, let's hear what you have to say."

Piper wasted no time lollygagging. She assumed her position at the front of the room with an air of utmost confidence. She delved in deep, using her charts, graphs, and numbers to support her endorsement. Her due diligence even managed to impress Jan who was by far the hardest nut to crack. Piper's reluctance to veer from her rehearsed script caused her to stumble when Chuck caught her off-guard with one of his questions. With the help of Carolyn, she was able to regain her composure and finish the presentation without any other noticeable mishaps.

"To be clear," Rev. Black began, "you are recommending a major reduction to the retirement benefits as well as the healthcare plans?"

Piper replied, "That is correct. I realize it's not the popular choice, but I truly believe it's our fiduciary responsibility to do what's best for the future of the library. I wish there was an alternative, but the numbers don't lie."

"Yes, but this decision will greatly impact the livelihood of our dedicated employees. I, for one, see no other choice but to reject this recommendation. Personally, I think it's a grave injustice." His theatrical grandstanding pleased those in the rear whose angry whispers echoed around the room.

Piper kept her composure despite the obvious tension in the room. "I applaud your unwavering support for our employees. I, too, hold them in the highest esteem. But as board members, we are called upon to make the hard decisions for the good of the organization as a whole. Reverend Black, I suggest you take a step back and look at the bigger picture. Don't allow your personal feelings to cloud your judgment."

The veracity of Piper's statement rang true with the other board members whose deafening silence spoke volumes. Reverend Black's plan to sabotage Piper's recommendation failed miserably. What could have been a titanic struggle among the diverse group of board members turned into a mutual acceptance of what must be for the library's sustainability.

Judge Halbreath called for a motion, which January presented with little fanfare. Carolyn stepped in to second the motion. As Mrs. B. called the roll, one by one the members of the board of trustees voted 'aye' save Reverend Black who melodically bellowed 'nay'. At the end of the meeting, Judge Halbreath asked for comments from the public. Rather than voice their displeasure, Mrs. Johnson and her cronies exited the room. In the bigger scheme of things, the employees accepted the fact that times were a-changing much to their displeasure. The meeting was adjourned for the night.

Larry gathered his belongings and then headed over towards Piper. "Good job, Piper. I hate to admit it, but job well done. I honestly didn't think you were up to the task. I guess it's true…looks can be deceiving."

"Isn't that the truth? Now if I only could figure out who killed Brandt." Her comment underscored the irony of the situation.

Larry gave her a faint nod, choosing not to comment any further. He politely excused himself and then made his way over to the other side of the room to confer with his muse, Desiree. The two cozied up in the corner talking privately away from the others.

Piper stood riveted to the spot while observing the two deep in conversation. On repeated occasions, Desiree reached out and gently touched Larry's arm, hands, or shoulder. She even threw her head back in a flirtatious manner when laughing. Not typical behavior from someone who claimed to be repulsed by his presence. If Piper didn't know any better, she'd wager a guess those two were sleeping together.

"Are you just going to stand there all night?" a voice interrupted her train of thought.

"Oh, Mrs. B.! I didn't realize that I was blocking the aisle. My apologies!" Piper moved aside.

The woman stood tall with a thick stack of notepads, files, and papers up against her chest.

"Would you like some help?" Piper offered a hand.

Mrs. B. opened her lips as if to say something but then changed her mind.

"Here!" Piper said. "Let me help lighten your load." She reached for the top stack of papers.

"No!" Mrs. B. insisted. She pulled away. "You've done quite enough already. I'm more than capable of handling this on my own." She pushed ahead, leaving Piper wondering whether this atypical behavior was a direct result of the vote.

Piper's phone beeped, alerting her to an incoming text. Still shaken by Mrs. B.'s obvious brush-off, she hastily withdrew it from her purse.

Where r u?

Typing a quick reply, she answered Jay's question…
Library

Meet me in parking lot.

Piper accepted his request… *K*

All of a sudden, the room became eerily silent. The lights dimmed as Piper scurried toward the exit. The others had departed, leaving Piper the last to exit the room. Near the doorway, she found the light switch. As soon as she crossed the threshold, she turned off the lights and then closed the door.

Piper walked down the hallway towards the common area. Last minute stragglers were congregating near the check-out desk to claim their literary finds. Mrs. Johnson kept the line moving with her efficient pace. Rarely did an item slip by without her properly checking it out. The woman was better than a well-oiled machine for she knew every aspect of the library system like the back of her hand. No one dared to question her, a well-known fact acknowledged among the seasoned employees. As Piper made her approach, Mrs. Johnson peered up over her spectacles. When her sight set upon Piper, she quickly averted her gaze to continue her job at hand. Mrs. Johnson's rash decision to disregard Piper unnerved her for a brief moment. Piper paused to debate whether she should make a point of going over to say hello. Having just experienced Mrs. B.'s frigid reaction, Piper erred on the side of caution and whisked by the desk in pursuit of Jay.

The parking lot contained a small number of cars due to the time of night. With darkness looming, it was difficult for Piper to locate Jay among the vehicles. Rather than mill about risking a spill onto the pavement, Piper headed over to the area where she had earlier parked her car. Sure enough, sitting on top of the hood, she found Jay chomping down on a slice of pizza with a bottle of cheap beer firmly in hand.

"Are you crazy?" Piper shouted. She quickened her step. "Put that bottle down right now," she whispered. "You can't be in a public place swigging a beer, you moron." As soon as Piper encroached on his personal space, she could tell there was going to be trouble. "You're drunk as a skunk!" She looked around to see if anyone was within earshot. Luckily, they were by themselves in the side lot.

"That's what she said," Jay answered.

"Ha, ha," Piper sighed. "Now is not the time for humor. I need to get you home to bed."

Jay sat up straighter. "No, seriously, that's what Suzy said. She kicked me out of the diner and told me to go sleep it off."

Piper placed her arm around Jay to help guide him off the hood of her precious car. "Maybe you should have listened to her, pal. Why the heck did you drag yourself over here to the library?" Piper stole the pizza out of his hand and helped herself to a bite. "Good pizza, by the way. Where did you get it?" She handed it back to him as she opened the car door.

He shoved it back into her face. "No, you eat it. I feel like I'm going to get sick."

Piper quickly slammed the door shut and then tossed the slice of pizza into the bushes. Carefully, the two friends sat down on the curb. "Put your head between your legs just in case, well...it'll make you feel better. Just do it." Piper peeked over the hood of the car to see if anyone was in the vicinity. Luckily, their corner of the parking lot remained vacant. She resumed her position by his side.

Jay started to cry. "All I wanted to do was warn her about her grandmother getting arrested, but she never gave me the chance to tell her. I'm a good guy. Right, Piper?" He threw his arms around Piper and held her in a tight embrace.

"Whoa, slow down there, partner. Whose grandmother is getting arrested?" Piper was confused. The couple rocked back and forth. "You're spewing mumbo jumbo. Relax, buddy." She tenderly rubbed Jay's back to try to calm him down.

"Capt. Morgan stopped by. He was pooping for blues," he rambled.

"You mean snooping for clues, dear." Piper corrected him.

"That's what I said," he hiccupped into her ear.

Piper withdrew herself from his embrace and looked Jay straight in the eyes. "Concentrate," she told him. "What exactly did Capt. Morgan tell you, Jay?"

Jay snickered. "Did you know he's named after a brand of vodka?"

"Rum," Piper insisted.

"I don't think so," he swayed left, then right, and then collapsed back into Piper's arms.

"Darn it, Jay! Don't pass out on me!" Piper pleaded.

"I'm tired, Piper." His wan smile faded.

Piper gently laid him back down in the grass. She grabbed her phone from her purse and called Rusty. Her rapid fire recap provided enough information for him to get the gist of what was going on. As expected, Rusty assured her help was on its way.

True to his word, Rusty swerved into the parking lot at the helm of his manly truck. He pulled up right beside Piper's vehicle and jumped out of the cab.

"What do we have here?" Rusty surveyed the area. The sleeping lush was snoring loudly as he lay in the fetal position nestled in the grass.

"I don't know where to start," she heaved a sigh. "Let me just fast forward to the end. Jay was on the verge of telling me that he somehow knows who the murderer is. Evidently, your step-father told him? Then in true Jay fashion, he passed out cold. Go figure." Piper threw her hands up in the air.

"Grab his feet. Let me see if I can hoist him up here. For a skinny dude, he sure weighs a ton." With minimal assistance from Piper, Rusty was able to heave Jay over his right shoulder and then load him into the bed of his truck. "Not the most comfortable position, but it'll do for now." Jay curled up on his side with drool slowly escaping from the side of his mouth. "Do you happen to have a key to Jay's apartment, or should I just meet you at our house?"

Piper responded, "*My* house in five." She wasn't quite ready to give up partial ownership even if she was only steps away from the altar.

Not long after, the couple sat on the couch recounting the events that led up to Jay's drunken episode. For the most part, Jay remained unresponsive save a couple outbursts here and there. As the clock approached midnight, Piper and Rusty checked on him one last time before starting their retreat to the master bedroom for the night.

"I guess we'll have to wait until morning to pump Mr. Sleeping Beauty here for the details," Rusty tousled Jay's unruly mane.

"Are you sure we can't call Capt. Morgan?" Piper pleaded.

Rusty reached for her hand. "What part of he doesn't want you sticking your nose into the investigation don't you get?" He gently kissed the top of her blonde-haired head.

Piper grinned. "That's never deterred me before."

"C'mon, sleepy head. We both could use a good night's sleep." He tugged her towards the staircase. "Cinderella must get rid of those bags under her eyes for tomorrow night's ball," Rusty chided her.

Piper's revealing expression said it all. She couldn't jog up the stairs fast enough.

Meanwhile across town, the murderer couldn't sleep a wink. Tossing and turning, the thought of what lay ahead caused hours of sleeplessness mixed with worry. Yet, the one reassuring fact that kept the villain at peace was the realization that tomorrow night she finally had a chance. To rid herself of Ms. Know-it-all Piper O'Donnell once and for all without fear of being caught was all the incentive she needed to gradually close her eyes and dream.

Chapter 18
Booklovers' Ball: Art & Sold

The nagging sound of the alarm clock awakened Piper from a deep sleep. Blinded by the morning sun, she felt around on the nightstand until she was able to silence the buzzer. Piper turned over to her left side fully expecting to fall into the tender arms of her lover. Imagine her surprise when instead she rolled on top of her temperamental feline in search of his morning vittles.

"Okay, okay!" Piper insisted. "Pipe down, little man. I need a moment." The pounding of her head and uneasiness of her stomach did not bode well for the taxing day ahead. After some gentle kneading from her kitty, Piper found the energy to emerge from her king-sized bed in search of a morning meal for two. Down in the kitchen, she poured some seafood crunchies into Ralph Lauren's favorite blue dish. The little motorboat purred with delight with Piper's choice for breakfast. For herself, she settled on some crunchy granola and a cup of decaf coffee to decompress. Piper wasn't the least bit surprised to be feeling off-kilter on the cusp of such an important event. Perhaps a little yoga would do the trick to bring her back to Zen.

Just then Piper's cell phone buzzed. Never mind the yoga. A frantic call from Carolyn redirected Piper's woes. January and "the queen of social correctness" were in the throes of a heated argument over which party favors to use since evidently two different motifs were ordered by accident. In typical Piper fashion, she came to the rescue with a simple modification incorporating both patterns.

As soon as she hung up, the phone rang once again. This time Desiree was on the line with a ticket issue. Some V.I.P. claimed to have ordered four tickets, not two like he'd received in the mail. Since the event was at full capacity, Desiree needed guidance in solving this tricky situation. One after another, problems kept popping up in need of Piper's attention. The constant demand on her time prevented her from reaching out to Rusty or Jay. Not knowing who Capt. Morgan thought was responsible for Brandt's murder was figuratively killing her. Despite her frustration, the murder investigation had to be put on hold for the time being. The Booklovers' Ball needed her full devotion.

When noontime rolled around, Piper resigned herself to a self-imposed timeout to recharge her drained batteries. To avoid being interrupted, she flipped her phone to silent and cozied up on the couch with her much loved leopard print blanket. It didn't take long for her to doze off as her customary stamina waned.

The clanging of pots and pans roused Piper from her mid-day siesta. She sneaked a casual peek at her smartphone and gasped in horror when she realized it was nearly four o'clock in the afternoon. "Hello?" she cried out. "Who's making that thunderous racket in my kitchen?" Piper dragged her tired body from the sofa in search of the commotion.

"Hey there, sleepyhead! Feeling better?" Rusty opened his arms wide, inviting her into his warm embrace.

Piper snuggled up close and rested her head on his shoulder. "I don't know what's up with me. I've been feeling exhausted lately." She stifled a yawn.

He brushed a few wisps of blonde hair from her eyes. "I don't know what to tell you, babe. But, you don't have time to worry about it now. Penelope just called. She'll be here soon. You both have your hair appointments at the salon," he reminded her.

"But, what about Suzy and her grandmother? Were you able to get anything more out of Jay?" Piper was anxious for news.

"Not from Jay, but I did talk with Capt. Morgan," he teased.

"Well? Don't leave me hanging." Piper broke free from his embrace.

"Evidently, Mrs. B. and Suzy are related." Rusty dropped the proverbial bomb.

"Get out!" she shouted. "Now this all makes sense." Piper had a sudden burst of energy. "Mrs. B. did kill Brandt, and I can prove it. She acted all sunny and seventy-five towards me when I was passed out cold on the floor in Brandt's office. Yet when the time came for me to make my recommendations for the retirement and healthcare plans, she changed her tune. I can't believe I fell for it. Shame on me!"

Rusty weighed the options. "It could be plausible. Or maybe she knows who did it."

Piper continued. "No, no. Listen to me. Brandt had the power to screw up her nest egg. With him out of the picture, Mrs. B. thought she had averted a financial disaster. Then I come along and pick up where he left off."

Rusty said, "Hmm. But to kill him…"

"Maybe it was an accident. Maybe she just meant to scare him straight." Piper thought aloud.

"If what you're saying is true…"

"About her killing Brandt? Yes, I *know* it is," she clarified.

"And evidently, so does my step-dad. If he didn't, she wouldn't be his prime suspect. I guess we need to come up with an ingenious plan to get Mrs. B. to confess at the ball without Capt. Morgan realizing we are interfering with his investigation. Any ideas?" Rusty scratched his head.

At that moment, the front door was flung open and in walked Penelope. "I've been beeping the horn for the last five minutes. What are you two doing in here?"

Rusty started to explain, but Penelope cut him off mid-sentence.

"On second thought, I don't need to know. The bus is pulling out, sis. You have three minutes." A quick once-over prompted Penelope to rag on her big sis. "Really? You might want to go throw something else on. You're down to two minutes and counting..." she shouted while parading out the front door.

Piper followed her sister's advice by rummaging through the dryer in search of some clean clothes. "A bit wrinkled, but this will do." She threw on a pair of cropped jeans and a blue nautical striped shirt. "No one will know I wore this yesterday."

Rusty gave her the thumbs-up.

"You stay here and come up with something. I'll be back in an hour." She blew him a kiss.

"What's my incentive?" He egged her on.

Piper gave him a wink and then disappeared out the door.

Despite the maddening crowd at the salon, the sisters finagled a way to get in and out within the allotted forty-five minutes as planned. Following their primping session, they made a mad dash back to Piper's in order to change into their gowns. As luck would have it, they managed to have a spare fifteen minutes to take a breather before Reverend Black pulled up promptly in the back of a stretch limousine at five thirty. At the last minute, Jay and Suzy opted to drive separately leaving the sisters and their handsome beaus to toast to the marvelous evening ahead as the driver took them along the back roads leading up to the impressive estate.

"Wait until you see the magnificent artwork your sister selected for the auction!" Reverend Black complimented his date. "No doubt, this woman has good taste."

Piper gagged on her sparkling water in response to his attempt to impress her.

"Don't mind her." Rusty tried to cover for Piper's guffaw. "Acid reflux."

Piper rolled her eyes.

Rusty slipped his cell phone into Piper's purse. "Please hold onto it for me in case I have a few too many drinks," he explained.

"The who's who of Woodlawn will be here tonight. A sold-out crowd," the reverend commented.

"I'm looking forward to seeing Brandt's murderer," Piper said matter-of-factly.

A spritz of champagne spewed from Rusty's mouth which landed on the sleeve of Reverend Black's tuxedo.

"So, Stephen." Piper tried to divert his attention. "How's the church business going?"

"Any new benefactors? You know, to help alleviate the debt issue," Rusty added.

Piper leveled her fiancé with an evil stare.

Penelope joined in on the conversation. "I, for one, am looking forward to hanging out with Jay and Suzy in the VIP area." She lightly kicked Piper on the shin as a warning sign to behave or else.

Piper responded with a make-shift smile.

For the remainder of the thirty-minute car ride, the two couples chitchatted about neutral topics. Penelope made a point of keeping a tight rein on her sister by commandeering the conversation. When the venue finally came into view, Penelope released a sigh of relief. She was fed up with her sister's silly antics and told her so in private once they exited the limo. The two couples parted ways each with their own agenda for the night.

"That didn't go so well, huh?" Piper laced her arm through Rusty's. The striking couple moseyed along in the same direction as the crowd.

He shook his head no. "Not our finest moment, babe. Let's hope we do better trapping a murderer."

Piper leaned over and planted a kiss on his cheek.

In return, he squeezed her hand in support.

The multitude of guests filled the old mansion with snippets of conversation and giggles of laughter. The folks of Woodlawn displayed their finery as they sipped cocktails while admiring the eclectic display of artwork. The tolling of the grandfather clocked signified the official start to the event as the VIPs sated their appetites with a smattering of hors d'oeuvres.

Piper kept a watchful eye on the front door, noting the arrival of certain key individuals. As expected, members of the board of trustees were among the first to cross the threshold along with their significant others where apropos. Piper and Rusty positioned themselves near the periphery to observe the lively gathering from a safe distance.

At precisely seven o'clock, the general public gained access to the venue. The next round of specialty drinks and appetizers were offered to the newcomers. Music energized the room as people swayed to the tempo while sampling fruity concoctions with friends.

With her stomach in knots, Piper passed on the trendy cocktails and opted for a plain ginger ale in its place. Rusty, on the other hand, downed one drink after another, claiming to need the booze to get the conversation flowing. The couple drifted from one circle of acquaintances to the next, chatting up their contemporaries in an effort to blend in with the surroundings. All the while, Piper continued to scour the room in search of the prime suspect.

Drawing near to the end of the cocktail hour, Capt. Morgan waltzed into the grand foyer pushing his wife Helen's wheelchair. Piper and Rusty tried to avoid them by engaging in a superfluous conversation with a high profile donor, but were soon thwarted as Capt. Morgan and Helen inserted themselves into the conversation. It didn't take long for Capt. Morgan to drag Piper and his step-son aside to find out exactly what sordid activity the scheming pair was conspiring to commit.

"If you bungle my investigation, I will hightail both of you down to the station and arrest you for interfering with official police work. You got that?" Capt. Morgan didn't mince words. Related or not, he meant business.

"We plan to adhere to your sage advice and enjoy the evening," Piper assured him. To make herself feel better for lying, she crossed her fingers behind her back.

Capt. Morgan continued to admonish the couple, but his cautionary litany fell on deaf ears. For out of the corner of Piper's eye, she spotted Mrs. B. entering the room with Mrs. Johnson following closely behind. Simultaneously, the chimes tolled eight o'clock, the opening of the silent auction. The crowd was ushered towards the rear of the building where the majority of the paintings hung on display. Capt. Morgan, Helen, and Rusty were swept away among the throng of partygoers, leaving Piper lagging behind with the wait staff who were in the midst of collecting the discarded glasses and plates.

"Ditch your date?" A gentleman's voice sounded from afar.

Piper spun around to find Larry leaning against the doorframe of the adjoining library.

"I figured it was just a matter of time. The two of you are a mismatched pair, to say the least." His wicked smile leered at her.

Piper closed the gap between them by advancing a few steps in his direction. "I don't recall asking for your opinion."

Larry altered his approach.

"It's such a shame Brandt's not here to witness this magnificent affair. Did you happen to see Shep? He's milling about like a lost soul. Poor guy." Larry paused for a moment and then said, "Join me in the library for a snifter of brandy?"

"I suppose." Piper had a hunch Larry's veiled remark concerning Brandt and Shep might lead to something more consequential. For that reason alone, she was willing to throw one back despite her distaste for hard liquor.

The library was situated off the main hall tucked in between the dining room and the parlor. Even though it was springtime, a roaring fire was lit to chase the nighttime chill away. Two club chairs flanked the hearth with a carved mahogany side table placed in the middle. Larry went ahead and poured the drinks while Piper relaxed in front of the fireplace.

"I see Capt. Morgan is in attendance this evening. Any updates on the case?" Larry handed Piper a snifter of brandy. He assumed his position in the opposite facing chair.

"Your guess is as good as mine. We don't talk shop at family dinners." Piper swirled her drink, but neglected to take a sip.

"C'mon, Piper. You must have a hunch." His lame attempt to pry her for information got him nowhere.

"So, I guess you and Mrs. B. are thick as thieves," Piper tossed him a bone of sorts.

"Not especially," he commented.

Piper watched as Larry sniffed and swirled his drink before indulging in a generous sip. "That surprises me, seeing as she's worked at the library for many years. I'd think she would be a valuable resource for you as well as a trusted confidant." Piper pursed her lips on the rim of the glass as if taking a sip. As soon as Larry began to talk, she nonchalantly moved the glass to the side table.

"Mrs. B. and I have had our issues. I feel no shame in saying that her retirement couldn't come soon enough. She needs to be put out to pasture." He finished off his drink.

"There you are!" a familiar voice shouted. "I've been searching all over this house for you. Look at you! Stand up! Let me take a gander at that gorgeous gown."

Piper passed on the opportunity to respond to Larry's comment concerning his abhorrence for his subordinate. Instead she jumped on the Jay bandwagon which arrived in the nick of time.

"Spin around, Piper. I want to see that beautiful dress from every angle. It fits you like a glove." Jay's tunnel vision focused solely on Piper.

Feeling a bit out of place, Larry rose up from his chair and said, "I'll catch up with you later," and awkwardly left the room.

As soon as he was out of earshot, Jay said, "Spill it. I don't have much time. I need to get back to Suzy. Did you get anything out of him worth knowing?"

Piper passed her snifter of brandy to Jay who was more than happy to take a swig of the expensive alcohol.

"He despises Mrs. B., but so what? She didn't kill him," Piper reasoned aloud.

"Not yet," Jay quipped.

"What did you say?" Piper stared him in the face.

Jay swallowed the last drop of liquor in the glass and then answered, "I said not yet. Why?"

Piper replied, "That's it! Hear me out. Both Larry and Brandt agreed that the budget needed to be trimmed starting with the healthcare and retirement benefits. Maybe Brandt was in Larry's office fishing around for some paperwork…"

"And, Mrs. B. came in and shut the door," Jay filled in her sentence.

"Exactly! The two got into a heated argument…" Piper teetered back and forth on her strappy high heels.

"And, Mrs. B. squashed him with the bookcase to make a point?" Jay speculated.

Piper shook her head no. "I think it was an accident. I think she didn't mean to do him any harm. She probably thought she could talk some sense into him, and it backfired. Mrs. B. has given her heart and soul to the library for the majority of her life. She probably feels betrayed by the board for taking away money that she has rightfully earned. "

Jay sat down in the club chair. "So, now what?"

Piper stood tall. "We need to get her to confess before she does something foolish like go after Larry. Take my word for it. Those two have been at each other's throats lately. If she admits it was an accident, her lawyer might be able to convince the judge to give her a lighter sentence."

"Good luck with that! The old lady is not doing time. She's smarter than a coonhound on a hunt. Mrs. B. will sniff you out." Jay wasn't having it.

"C'mon." Piper grabbed hold of Jay's forearm. "Follow me."

Piper and Jay made their way through the crowd keeping a watchful eye for any signs of Mrs. B. Along the back foyer, a bunch of older gents congregated in front of a cluster of bucolic paintings. As Piper and Jay attempted to bypass the group, one painting in particular caught Piper's eye, causing her to come to a complete stop. Following closely on her heels, Jay had no choice but to collide with Piper's skull.

"Ouch!" he exclaimed while rubbing his bruised forehead. "Rusty wasn't joking. You do have a hard head."

Piper disregarded his comment for she was more interested in the familiar painting on display. "Excuse me," she asked one of the men. "Would you happen to know anything about this painting?" She pointed at the canvas in question.

"Ah, you mean Chuck Loudon's feeble attempt at becoming an artist?" the gruff older gentleman replied. The others cackled at the mention of Chuck's name.

Immediately, Piper recalled where she'd seen it...stuffed in a back hall at the hardware store. Piper's admiration and sense of allegiance for her library colleague gave her the nerve to say, "You gents might want to get your bids in now. I heard a rumor some famous art collector from New York City has expressed interest in this very collection. These paintings are going to be worth big bucks one day. Just don't tell anyone I let you in on the secret."

Piper's so-called secret revelation instantly squashed the crass comments coming from the old cronies. As she and Jay walked away, Piper could hear them whispering among themselves something about pooling their money together in order to secure the artwork. As far as Piper was concerned, her little white lie was a win-win for both the library and Chuck's self-esteem. It was the least she could do for her friend.

Meanwhile, Reverend Black had assumed his position as emcee for the night. He seemed to have managed to write his own script without Piper's help, she noted. His booming voice could be heard above the chatter as he introduced the names of those individuals responsible for coordinating the evening. The deafening sound of applause coupled with the hordes of people lingering near the food stations caused Piper and Jay to break off and search on their own in an effort to save time. Jay also needed to check in with his date. Piper paused briefly when her name was called and waved at the crowd in acknowledgment. She then continued along in hot pursuit of the missing suspect. She realized not much time remained before the closing of the silent auction at nine. Piper quickened her step as she navigated the swarm of guests.

Outside on the veranda, Piper bumped into Carolyn and Judge Halbreath.

"There you are, Piper. Your ears must have been burning. I was just telling Judge Halbreath about your desire to take selfies from this vantage point. Where's that hunk of yours?"

Piper surveyed the area and came up empty-handed. "I was asking myself that very same question. It's been over an hour since I laid eyes on him. Maybe he's chatting with Mrs. B. over at the bar."

"Oh, no," said Carolyn. "I ran into Mrs. B. about ten minutes ago upstairs in the coat check overflow. She was taking to task some poor teenager who left a mink coat lying on the floor. In return, the young lady was educating her concerning the atrocity of the senseless killing of animals for vanity's sake. Truth be told, my money is on the teenager to win that argument." Carolyn burst into laughter.

Piper nodded in agreement and smiled. She then politely excused herself to go in search of Rusty among the partygoers. Due to the host of attendees clogging up the hallways, it was necessary for Piper to weave in and out of the crowd, often having to wait until space opened up to pass. By the time she made it to the front entrance, the clock nearly approached eight thirty. At the base of the staircase, Penelope and Reverend Black stood in line waiting to have their photo snapped by the party pic guy. At first, Piper intended to zip by without acknowledging the couple's presence, but then she thought better of it.

"Hey, sis!" Piper tested her sister's annoyance level.

"No, you can't cut in line." Penelope reacted firmly and to the point. "Besides, it's taking forever. The committee really should have hired two photographers."

Piper quipped, "Good to know." She directed her next comment to the minister. "Stephen, you're a natural emcee. Such poise and command over the audience. We must touch base later on concerning my upcoming fundraiser hosted by The Cardinal Shoppe." Her attempt to stroke the reverend's inflated ego proved to be successful.

"Why thank you, Piper. I'd be happy to lend my services to your charity function." He beamed with sheer delight.

The line inched ahead.

"Excuse me, do you mind if I cut through here? I left something in the pocket of my coat." She pointed upstairs.

"You didn't wear a coat, Piper." Penelope flatly denied the statement. "And, you're carrying a purse."

"Oh, I meant to say Carolyn's coat. I asked her to hold onto my raffle ticket." Piper exchanged a knowing glance with her little sister. As expected, Penelope honored the sister code by keeping quiet rather than calling her out as a big, fat liar in front of the reverend. Piper thanked her for stepping aside, and promised to meet up with the couple at the close of the silent auction at nine.

With little time to spare, Piper sprinted up the first few steps; however, her sparkly shoes slowed her down since the old, creaky boards were warped in certain places. When she reached the top of the staircase, she paused for a moment to catch her breath. While admiring the beauty of the antiquated grandfather clock, she grabbed hold of the banister in order to adjust her shoe strap. The structure gave way a bit causing Piper to move away for fear of falling. The minutes ticked by signaling a sense of urgency for Piper to find Mrs. B. before it was too late.

Piper tiptoed along the hallway peeking into the darkened rooms. The eerie sound of stillness prickled the hairs on the back of her neck. Towards the end of the hallway, she spotted a faint light shining from within a doorframe. Like a moth to a flame, she quickened her pace. When she crossed the threshold, Piper noticed a few coat racks stuffed with light dress coats. She breathed a sigh of relief for she'd finally found the overflow room. Piper shouted hello a couple of times, but Mrs. B. did not answer. In fact, no one said a word for the room was left unattended.

"Darn it!" Piper winced in pain from the constant friction of her fancy stilettos. Sure enough, a blister had begun to form in the exact same spot where she'd had one before. In need of a temporary reprieve, she removed both shoes and slung them on a vacant chair. Piper pulled a phone out from her purse and sent Jay a text alerting him to her whereabouts. As she waited for him to reply, she perused the assemblage of outerwear stashed in the room.

"Uh, hmm," the sound of someone clearing his or her throat caught Piper's attention.

"Hello?" Piper said.

Standing in the doorway was Mrs. Johnson with a bunch of wooden hangers in her hands.

"Oh, Mrs. Johnson! What are you doing here?" Piper inquired. "Did you need a hanger for your coat?"

Mrs. Johnson brushed right by and dumped the pile onto a nearby desk. "No, dear. I'm stuck up here offering to hang up coats for party guests like you. My shift ends at eleven o'clock." Her glum expression did little to lighten the mood.

Piper walked barefoot over to where the librarian stood. "Really? I didn't realize you were working the event. I thought you said you'd bought a ticket."

The woman narrowed her gaze. "I sold it."

"Why would you do that?" Piper leaned up against the desk.

Mrs. Johnson said, "Thanks to you and Brandt, my spending money has been drastically reduced. I'll have to postpone my retirement for at least three more years. Then again, who knows? At the rate my retirement benefits keep shrinking, I may never stop working. All because you two took it upon yourselves to recommend to the board to take away what is rightfully mine!" The hostile woman seethed with anger.

Piper blurted out, "Did Mrs. B. convince you to do it?"

Mrs. Johnson picked up a hanger. "Do what? Push a bookcase over to squash the spineless wimp?"

Piper swallowed hard. "It must have been an accident. Did you two argue?"

"Argue?" Mrs. Johnson walked over to the door and closed it firmly shut. "There was nothing to argue about. His mind was made up and the recommendation was scheduled to go forward. All I did was tip the bookcase a little and splat! His skull was crushed in right at the temple. Not the most pleasant way to go, but he deserved it! I had been telling maintenance for months that Larry's bookcases needed to be anchored. See what happens when you don't listen to me. I was at my wit's end."

Piper maneuvered herself towards the window.

"You're going nowhere, Barbie Doll. I'm tired of people like you dictating how people like me should live." She tapped the hanger against the palm of her hand.

Piper scanned the room in search of something to use as a weapon. "How does Mrs. B. factor into this equation? Was she your accomplice?"

Mrs. Johnson expelled a sinister laugh. "Hardly. Yet your future father-in-law thinks she's responsible, so I'm willing to go along with that theory."

Piper inched away from her. "Something doesn't add up. Explain to me why you'd risk your own freedom to kill Brandt over some lousy retirement benefits. Unless…"

Mrs. Johnson waited for Piper to fit together the missing pieces.

"You're the one who pilfered the missing funds! Oh my gosh! And, Brandt figured it out! The board president was going to expose you to all of Woodlawn as a common criminal, so you killed him." Piper screeched as she began pacing back and forth in front of the window. "But, who took pity upon you? Who bailed you out? Was it Larry? Mrs. B.?" She stole a glance out the window hoping to find someone to help her.

"Manipulating Larry was child's play. Threatening to divulge his true sexuality was all the incentive he needed to help me come up with the dough, especially with Nancy breathing down his neck." Mrs. Johnson admitted.

"What do you mean by true sexuality?" Piper inquired.

Mrs. Johnson tossed Piper's shoes onto the floor and then planted herself in the chair. "I think I need to be seated for this. Must I explain everything to you? Larry and Shep have been secretly seeing each other. The two are an item."

Piper gasped.

"That's yesterday's news, my dear. Why do you think he was so flirtatious with Desiree and other single women at the library? Easiest way to dodge any suspicions. Nothing gets by me, Piper. Moving on! Now the question becomes what to do with you. I hadn't planned on killing you Piper, but it looks as though I have no other option. Of course, Mrs. B. will look guilty as hell seeing as everyone knows you were searching for her tonight. Let me think for a minute or two on how to go about getting this done." She leaned back in the chair and raised her legs up onto an empty egg crate.

At that moment, the gonging of the grandfather clock triggered Mrs. Johnson to stand at attention. "Yikes! It seems as though time is running out."

Piper grabbed Rusty's phone from her purse.

"Hand that over, missy. You don't have the option of phoning a friend." Mrs. Johnson marched over to where Piper was standing and snatched it from her grip. Mrs. Johnson debated for a brief moment as to what to do, and then opened the nearby window and tossed it out. She then slammed it shut.

"Do you have any idea how much that phone cost Rusty?" Piper scolded her while taking a few steps closer towards the woman.

"Doesn't matter," Mrs. Johnson informed her. "Where you're going, you can't take it with you." She laughed at her own comment.

Their attention turned to the commotion coming from the hallway. A demonstrative voice said, "It's not yours. The pink sparkly bling could only belong to one fabulously chic person...Piper O'Donnell. Pshaw with your finder's keepers dribble." Jay and a pimple-ridden teenager came barreling into the room. "Ah, ha! There she is!" Jay zeroed in on his dear friend Piper. "Let's ask her ourselves if this belongs to her."

Jay breezed right by Mrs. Johnson and directed his question to Piper. "Miss Baylor Swifty wannabe here is trying to lay claim to this bedazzled phone. I presume this is yours?" Jay slipped it into the palm of Piper's hand. His sassy tone was intended to irk his teenage companion.

"Taylor Swift," Piper corrected him. "And, yes! It's most certainly mine. I must have left it somewhere." She then proceeded to do the most logical thing in her situation. She sent off an SOS text to Capt. Morgan.

"Hold it right there!" Mrs. Johnson screamed. "No one move!"

The adolescent tart disregarded the flagrant warning and buzzed right out the door. "I'm outta here!" were her parting words to the crazy adults left behind in the room.

In true Jay fashion, he panicked. "Um, is there a problem here? Oh, yes. The coat I borrowed. I seem to have left it downstairs in the study. Let me go fetch it. I'll be right back." Jay bolted for the door only to be blocked by the formidable Mrs. Johnson, as intimidating as Piper and her sister waiting in line for the annual Lilly Pulitzer warehouse sale. He didn't dare cross her.

"As I tried to explain to your gal pal here, I need to figure out how to kill her. Little did I know I'd have two for one tonight!" Mrs. Johnson erupted into laughter.

Jay turned around and whispered to Piper. "I think she's bat shit crazy."

"No doubt." Piper agreed.

"Quiet!" Mrs. Johnson roared. "I need to concentrate." Right then, she removed a petite revolver from her purse. "I need to make sure I have enough bullets," she informed the pair.

Piper slowly rotated her body so that her back was facing Mrs. Johnson. She mouthed to Jay, "Move towards the window." Her plan to escape was put into place.

Jay replied aloud, "I know. It's stuffy in this room. Here." He handed her a flier he found on a side table. "Fan yourself with this."

Piper's eyes popped out of her sockets. Evidently, Jay didn't get the memo. A pamphlet wasn't the best weapon of choice for warding off a lunatic with a gun.

"What are you two knuckleheads up to over there?" Mrs. Johnson asked.

"Piper is sweating like a pig. If you don't mind, I'm just going to open this window to let some fresh nighttime air in." Jay traipsed over to unlatch the windowpane and then hoisted it open as far as it could go.

Mrs. Johnson rushed over trying to stop him. As soon as she was close enough, Jay gave her the heave ho and out the window she flew. Resting on the floor next to Jay's foot sat the lone revolver.

Down below, Reverend Black was in the middle of announcing the silent auction winners on the veranda when Mrs. Johnson's flailing body came crashing into the bubbling fountain. A giant swell of water doused Penelope who stood attentive by his side watching as the drama unfolded.

Upstairs, Piper and Jay scrambled down the hallway in an effort to catch the killer. Jay's long stride enabled him to pull ahead as Piper hopped along due to her painful blister. At the top of the stairs, Piper stubbed her toe causing her to trip. She tried to grab hold of the bannister, but the wobbly structure left her with no support. Within the blink of an eye, Piper came crashing down, landing in a heap at the bottom of the steps.

Rusty ran inside, parting the crowd with his muscular arms to get to his injured fiancée's side, all the while shouting, "Call 911!" On a bended knee, he caressed the side of her head trying to gauge the severity of her injuries. Piper moaned in pain as the sound of sirens blared in the distance.

"I don't feel well," Piper whined.

Rusty tried his best to keep her calm. "Sh! Just close your eyes and rest."

"I didn't get a piece of cake." Piper's penchant for sweets clouded her mind.

Rusty chuckled. "Neither did Mrs. Johnson."

Two sets of first responders suddenly appeared from the crowd and took charge of the situation. Within minutes they strapped Piper and Mrs. Johnson each to a stretcher and then wheeled them away to the waiting ambulances. The infamous Booklovers' Ball ended that fateful spring night with Piper uttering the words Rusty never expected to hear.

"Rusty?"

"I'm right here." He grabbed hold of her hand and then kissed the top of her head. "What's the matter?"

Piper gazed into his eyes and quietly whispered, "I think I'm pregnant."

Epilogue

"You have a visitor," the nurse informed Piper. "As soon as I finish up with your vital signs, I'll send him in."

Piper obliged the nurse's request by allowing her to perform the duties without interference. It had been less than twenty-four hours and so much had already changed. Piper placed her hands on her tummy in awe of the life growing inside of her. Two months pregnant without even knowing. Piper could only imagine what Rusty was thinking.

"All done," the nurse declared. "I would imagine the doc will send you home tomorrow morning. Mom and baby are doing just fine." Her caring smile warmed Piper's heart.

The nurse headed towards the door.

"My visitor?" Piper asked.

"Oh, yes. I almost forgot." She turned around to address her. "I'll send the gentleman right in."

"Thank you." Piper sat up a little straighter and adjusted her hospital gown to show a little cleavage. She didn't have much time to prep for her baby daddy, so she had to do the best with what she had. Piper tied her hair up in a messy ponytail and then applied a little lip balm. Voila! Her thirty-second make-over was complete.

"Well, I see you're feeling better," a man's voice startled her.

Piper looked over towards the door expecting to find her sexy fiancé. Instead, her soon-to-be father-in-law came strolling in with a bouquet of pink roses in hand.

"I brought you a peace offering." He held the flowers out in front of him.

Piper yanked the hospital blanket up under her chin to hide her voluptuous breasts from his view.

"I'll stick them over here on the radiator." He avoided making eye contact with her. "You might want to ask one of those pretty nurses to put them into a vase for you."

"Thank you." She relaxed a bit. "Have you seen Rusty?"

"He's over at the house with his mother. Helen's anxious to get the wedding plans started seeing as junior is already on the way. Evidently, the two of you need a refresher course on the birds and the bees." He raised his eyebrows.

Piper chose to brush over his pithy comment for the time being for she was far more interested in what happened after she'd left the ball.

"So, did you arrest Mrs. Johnson?" she inquired.

Capt. Morgan kept a comfortable distance from her by seating himself in the chair positioned at the foot of the bed. "Sure did. The hospital staff patched her up and then sent her over to the county jail. You made my job easy, Piper. The woman couldn't stop complaining about how you screwed up her life. She confessed the whole kit and caboodle right down to the part about blackmailing poor Larry Flagstone. I imagine she will be spending the remainder of her years behind bars."

"I told you my sister didn't kill Brandt." Piper reminded him.

Capt. Morgan nodded. "Yes, Piper. You were right. However, you deliberately disregarded my instructions to stay clear of my investigation. You're darn lucky Mrs. Johnson didn't harm you or the baby."

"Guilty as charged," she admitted. Piper eased back against the mattress.

"I can see you're getting tired. I need to return to the station anyway to complete some paperwork." He stood up ready to leave.

Piper said, "By the way, did you have a chance to speak with Mrs. B.? Did she have any idea what was going on?"

He responded, "She claims none, and I believe her. That woman doesn't have a mean bone in her body."

"I'm happy to hear she's innocent." Piper breathed a sigh of relief.

"This Booklovers' Ball of yours turned out to be quite the event. I'm sure people will be talking about it for years to come. Speaking of events, have you given any thought to the wedding? It's going to be a hard act to follow."

Piper answered, "As long as it doesn't involve a dead body, I'll be more than content."

ABOUT THE AUTHOR

 Jennifer Vido dishes the scoop on the latest happenings in the publishing business as the book editor at Momtrends.com. As a national board member and spokesperson for the Arthritis Foundation, she has been featured by *Lifetime Television, Redbook, Health Monitor, The New York Times, The Baltimore Sun, Healthguru.com,* and *Arthritis Today.* Currently, she lives in the Baltimore area with her husband and two sons. Visit her website at www.JenniferVido.com.